CHARLOTTE PHILLIPS

I live in Wiltshire, UK, where I squash writing in between looking after my family, who have been taught not to notice that I'm rubbish at housework. I love watching American TV shows in my pyjamas and I can't live without coffee and cake.

Did Someone Order Room Service?

CHARLOTTE PHILLIPS

Harper*Impulse* an imprint of
HarperCollins*Publishers* Ltd
77–85 Fulham Palace Road
Hammersmith, London W6 8JB

www.harpercollins.co.uk

A Paperback Original 2014

First published in Great Britain in ebook format by Harper*Impulse* 2013

A catalogue record for this book
is available from the British Library

ISBN: 978-0-00-755959-6

Automatically produced by Atomik ePublisher from Easypress

For Barry, who is always there for me.
With love and thanks.

CHAPTER ONE

Layla Jones wondered, not for the first time, if there could be such a thing as an entire-adult-life crisis instead of just a mid-life one.

She reached the top of the stairs and turned to walk at speed down the hotel's top floor corridor, heels sinking into the sumptuous ankle deep runner, phone clamped to her ear and eyes everywhere for the slightest sniff of another member of staff. Specifically anyone superior to her. Which actually amounted to quite a lot of people. Guest Services Agent was only a few steps above minion here at the Lavington Hotel. It had taken sixteen tries before her mother picked up the phone and she wasn't about to hit disconnect after all that effort just because of a little thing like personal phone use during work time.

Unfortunately this wasn't looking like a quick call since she apparently had to spell out the fact that what her so-called parent had done was unforgivable. She'd just have to dodge into a linen cupboard or something if push came to shove.

'I lent you my savings because you wanted to set up a business,' she said, and it sounded so laughable spoken out loud that she could scarcely believe she'd been so stupid. Her mother set up a business? In which universe would that be? 'And instead you've blown the lot on travel plans and concert tickets.'

'Don't be so dramatic, darling.' Behind her mother's attempt at soothing she could hear an airport tannoy announcing some flight or other. 'Chance of a lifetime this. Not just *any* concert tickets. This isn't some flash-in-the-pan manufactured cutesy boy band, you know. We're talking *Sweet Victory* here. Their comeback tour and I've got backstage passes. Did you hear me? Backstage Passes! *I'm with the band*, darling. I never missed one of their shows back in the Eighties and I'm not going to start now.'

Layla gripped the phone briefly away from her ear as she processed this information, and thought for a moment that she really must call up hotel maintenance to get the top floor air-con checked because it was suddenly *boiling* in here. Her mother had never missed one of their shows, oh no, she'd spent half Layla's childhood trailing around the world after them, wearing too much leather and hair mousse, while Layla outstayed her welcome with a progression of relatives.

Doors sped past, their glossy red number plates a blur. She didn't have time for this. She had an hour or so at best to check the Kerry Suite was prepared to perfection before the last-minute guests moved in. After that she'd have to keep a permanent can-I-help-you smile on her face as she saw to their every whim when what she wanted to do was snarl at everyone within shouting distance. She made an enormous effort to lower her voice.

'I was saving that money for a deposit on a flat,' she said. Finally it had felt within her grasp that she might actually be able to put down some roots of her own. Steady job and her own place instead of the tiny rented studio with its grotty shared bathroom and her mother kipping on the sofa for a few months at a time when she wasn't doing the festival season. 'You told me it was just a start-up thing. You promised you'd pay me back in a week or two when your bank loan came through.'

'And I *will* darling. Once the tour's over I'll be ready to get my teeth into that T-shirt business and you'll get your money back quick smart. Just a few months that's all.'

Layla mentally wrote off the cash. And when her mother turned up after this latest jaunt, just as she always did, murder might be on the cards.

'How the hell did I get stuck with you as a parent?' she wailed. 'Why can't you be like any *normal* mother? You should be teaching me how to make shortcrust pastry, handing down family recipes and lending *me* money to buy my first flat, not disappearing halfway round the world in a leather bustier and hair extensions.'

Her mother made a horrified noise.

'Sounds like a bloody boring nightmare to me. What are you, living in the dark ages?'

'No!' Layla spat. 'I'm living in the REAL WORLD!'

Temper completely lost now, she reached the end of the passageway and the door of the Kerry Suite with its red name plate. She flicked her pass card into the slot, threw open the door and stormed inside. The sitting room beyond was cool and quiet, October rain pattering softly against the high windows. The calm felt at odds with her scorching temper so she slammed the door hard enough to make the bottles in the mini-bar clink.

'You know what?' her mother's voice was smooth and clear on the end of the line, tinged now with more than a hint of offended temper. 'I'm not sure how the hell I got stuck with *you*.'

Layla paused, hand outstretched to reach the pad of light switches, her breath catching as her throat suddenly constricted.

'What do you think is more important?' her mother went on. 'Getting to work on time? Counting the pennies? Or living life to the full, taking in every unpredictable turn, feeling *alive*? No one ever laid on their death bed, Layla, and wished they'd put in a few more hours at the day job. Life is passing you by, do you know that? You'll get to old age, look back and realise you missed the whole bloody point.' There was a pause followed by a mutter, which felt somehow even worse because it sounded like her mother was thinking out loud now instead of talking to her. 'How can anyone so mind-numbingly dull share my gene pool? Sometimes

I wonder why I ever bother coming back.'

Anger and hurt seemed to boil upwards from Layla's toes to suffuse her whole body. Her pulse raced with it, her stomach churned with it and her lips pulled back from her teeth in a grimace of fury.

'Alright then,' she yelled, 'if that's the way you feel.' Her voice rose steadily in pitch until it was so loud that it cracked in her throat and she snarled into the phone like some hideous fishwife. 'Follow your saddo little groupie dream and DON'T BOTHER COMING BACK!'

She threw her arm back so far that her shoulder creaked and hurled the phone full-force across the semi-darkness of the room. There was a loud *BONK!* as it made contact with something on the other side of the couch and then it clattered to the floor beneath the flat screen TV.

'Oi!'

Layla clapped both hands to her mouth in shock as a man got to his feet, hand rubbing his forehead and mussing his dark hair into haphazard spikes. Tall, broad-shoulders, chiselled jaw and lop sided grin, which actually was currently more of a grimace but which still gave the chocolate brown eyes a hint of wicked melt. Instantly recognisable, even without the usual pro tennis kit.

'Let me guess,' he said, his American drawl audible now that he wasn't yelling. 'Room service?'

She'd just clobbered the biggest crowd-pull in world tennis. And she'd be lucky to end this day without the sack.

***

The light flush that touched her peaches and cream complexion and the knit of a frown above the china blue eyes elevated her from pretty to seriously cute, and Matt Stanton walked around the sofa to get a better look at her. She was staring at him with ill-disguised disbelief, but really, he was used to star-struck. It was a good look in his opinion, it meant anything was possible.

She took a calming breath and smoothed a stray tendril of blonde hair back into place where it curled softly into her neck.

'Guest Services,' she corrected, her voice pleasant and professional. She held up a clipboard. Her coarse snarling of five minutes earlier still hung in the air between them. 'My job is to make sure your stay runs as smoothly as possible.'

He stifled a laugh.

'Not got off to the greatest of starts then,' he said, rubbing his forehead.

She blushed again. He was beginning to enjoy the diversion. With the week of all-work-and-no-play that lay ahead of him it was an unexpected surprise. The phone had barely glanced off his head, but it would be *such* a shame to stop the show and point that out.

'Or perhaps knocking out the guest is always part of the package?' he said.

Worry flashed across her face as she made a panicky rush towards him.

'I'm SO sorry about that,' she said, stopping just shy of his personal space to stand on tiptoe and narrowing her eyes as she scrutinised his brow. He picked up a soft wave of her perfume, light and sweet, and his pulse jolted in response. 'I don't know what I was thinking. I just had a row, you know, *so* frustrating when you're not actually in the room with someone.' She shook her head, shrugged and smiled as if he must know exactly what she was talking about. His eyes zeroed in on her full upper lip, devoid of lipgloss but still absolutely delectable. 'Lost it for a second, just a split second.' She gazed at his forehead. 'It didn't break the skin, I can get you an ice pack if you like?'

She looked at him quizzically and he held up a hand to stop the mad stream of consciousness apology. She clenched her hands together and looked up at him beseechingly.

'Please don't report it. I know you have every right, but I'll get in so much trouble and I really…' she shook her head and lowered her voice to a level that smacked of desperation. '…I really need this job.'

In terms of boredom, the day had just taken a very interesting upswing. In the storm of press attention, before he'd been smuggled out of the country by his team, getting any female company had been impossible. A month now, by his standards practically a *drought*. Soon he would be reduced to gnawing the table. And then providence, fate, whatever it was, had lobbed her into his path. He instantly decided he would have her, not a question of whether he *could*, more a question of *how long* it would take him. A few hours maybe, if he played his cards right – that would be some kind of a record.

'Well, I just don't know,' he said, leaning in to get a better look at her name badge. 'My first stay in this particular hotel, hardly gives a good impression does it, Layla?'

Her face took on such a look of anguish that he couldn't stand it.

'Hey,' he said, as she clutched her hands in her blonde hair. 'I'm teasing. Chill out, of course I'm not going to report it. Anger, frustration, I can relate to that.'

He'd had his fair share of racquet throwing tantrums in the past, as his coach never tired of reminding him. Nothing wrong with a bit of fighting spirit and passion in his opinion. And as an added bonus, when it came to women there was a lot to be said for grabbing the upper hand when it presented itself.

He held up his hands.

'It never happened.'

'Omigod thank you SO much!'

She breathed out a massive audible sigh of relief and flung her arms around him. He breathed in the scent of her hair and took full advantage of the opportunity to slide a hand around her slender waist. The faint smell of her shampoo clung to her hair, something light with an edge of coconut that made him think of holidays.

'You're very welcome,' he whispered.

Layla jumped and disengaged herself from him with a quick pace backwards. What the hell was she *doing*, hugging the guests? Professional distance, that was the mantra peddled in all the training sessions. Then again, there were extenuating circumstances. It wasn't every day your mother spent your life savings on a stupid dream and you assaulted a celebrity with your mobile phone. Really, could she be expected to maintain professionalism under that kind of pressure? She felt his eyes on her as she straightened the dark skirt and jacket of her uniform and began to move around the room, plumping up velvet cushions and checking the mini-bar, each little task restoring an air of efficiency that would hopefully hide her fluster.

When she turned back to him he was leaning easily against the back of the sofa.

'Everything seems to be in order,' she said. 'Now my job is to make sure your stay runs as smoothly as possible. Any arrangements you might need, transport, food requests, laundry services, any problems at all, you can let me know.' She counted them off on her fingers. 'Nothing is too much trouble.'

'*Really*?' he said, eyebrow cocked, holding her gaze a beat too long. There was a predatory smile on his lips and her stomach gave a slow and very deliberate cartwheel. He somehow managed to communicate an entire proposition in that one word.

He moved back to the sitting room area and sat down on one of the berry coloured velvet sofas, slinging arms along the back of it that were twined with muscle and the most powerful shoulders she'd ever seen.

'Absolutely,' she said, heat rising in her cheeks. 'For the right guest at the right price, anything is doable. Room full of lilies? I'm your girl.'

'Glad to hear it,' he said. 'When you barged in here unannounced I assumed you were a fan. I didn't realise you were staff. I thought it was incredibly ironic, since I've been checked in here to stay away from them, that I'd ended up in the room with one.'

'I'm not a fan,' she said, then shrugged, 'well I mean, I *am*, the whole world is a fan of yours really isn't it? What I mean is, I've got my work hat on at the moment. Not my fan hat.'

Oh yes that sounded just bloody marvellous. Her cheeks burned as she caught the bemused expression on his face because he obviously thought she was saying that for effect, and in actual fact she'd blown her food shopping budget for a month on tickets to watch him play at Wimbledon the previous year. She was as smitten by him as the rest of the universe.

He was even hotter up close. Not that she'd thought that possible at the time. In all-white lawn tennis gear, with sweat tousling his dark hair and his lean muscular frame he'd been absolutely mesmerising.

And of course that had no bearing on the present. Dreaming about hot celebrities was one thing. Pure fantasy. The real world was a totally different ballgame. And unlike her mother Layla had no trouble keeping the two things separate.

'I really must apologise that I wasn't on hand for your arrival,' she said. 'I wasn't expecting you quite yet.'

There had been a rushed meeting this morning to discuss and fine-tune the details of his last minute booking with them. It was standard practice when dealing with a guest as high profile as America's tennis hero Matt Stanton. But when her shift had started this evening she'd been so busy getting out of earshot of the management and preoccupied with tracking down her mother that she'd come straight up to check the room the moment she arrived. As a result she'd missed any last minute schedule changes.

'My people called ahead and circumvented check-in,' he said. 'I just came straight up here.'

'And have you been shown around?'

It was somehow easier to deal with him when she kept herself in work mode. All those tried-and-tested and often-repeated stock hospitality phrases felt comfortingly familiar. She could hold her own when she was in work mode. Prided herself on it, actually, which was why the phone-throwing debacle was particularly toe-curling.

'I can work out how to work the flat-screen TV and the hot tub controls, if that's what you mean,' he said. 'I'm a veteran of hotel stays, I could probably even show you a thing or two.' Matt glanced across the room at the mod-cons. 'If it's any consolation I only found out I was going to be staying here myself a few hours ago.'

The curt discussion with his coach flashed back through his mind, accompanied by a twinge of resentment, and his mood darkened a little. Last week's big kiss 'n' tell revelation in the gossip columns, so close on the heels of the last one but this time backed up by blurry but perfectly recognisable mobile phone pictures, had combined with his recent slip in playing form to make his sponsors antsy and his management livid. They'd taken advantage of a break between tournaments to assert some authority while they reassessed his coaching. A time-out in London was the apparent solution. And not the kind of time-out he usually enjoyed.

The tennis circuit allowed for precious little downtime and the humiliation of being packed off to a lesser-known London boutique hotel instead of a swanky five-star celebrity choice, along with the list of instructions to stay out of sight, keep to his hotel suite when not training, no partying, no girls, no socialising, no damned *life*, had brought on a hot surge of angry rebellion. He might have succumbed on the hotel choice, but that didn't mean he had to give in on the rest of it – right? And a hot against-the-ludicrous-rules fling would be just the thing to prove he still had a stake in his own life, since just now it felt like every damned aspect of it was being controlled by someone else.

'Have a drink with me,' he said standing up and crossing the room to the mini-bar. 'It's past seven, I'm stuck in for the evening, might as well make the most of it.'

He gestured back at the two velvet sofas, facing each other over a low table. She didn't move, simply hovered by the door with her damn clipboard held up in front of her.

'I'm supposed to be working,' she said.

'Didn't you just get through telling me that *I'm* pretty much your job?' he said. 'If I want something, you're meant to arrange it – is that how it works?'

'Socialising with the guests isn't really allowed.'

'Even if the guest in question has requested your company? Even after you stumbled into their room without knocking and threw a telephone at their head?'

He saw a faint smile touch her lips and sensed her weakening even before she spoke. Of course she was weakening, they always did.

'Just an orange juice then,' she said.

Play it right and he could have her by the end of the day.

CHAPTER TWO

Layla walked over to the sofa and perched on the edge of it, keeping her clipboard on her lap. He crossed the room and handed her the juice. She watched as he poured himself a mineral water.

She stared at the glass in his hand.

'Mineral water,' she said.

'What of it?'

She shrugged.

'I just thought your drink of choice would be something a bit stronger. Mineral water doesn't exactly say hellraiser, does it?'

He grinned as he sat down opposite her and raised his glass.

'Neither does orange juice. We're perfect for each other.'

The blush was back. She looked down at her glass and he checked her left hand with the briefest glance. Always best to size up the conquest before he started out, and in his experience single girls caused the least trouble. And trouble right now was the last thing he needed.

No ring. Heat began to course through his veins as he looked at her, the full upper lip, the graceful curve of her neck highlighted by the curl of her blonde hair just below the jawline.

'That's different,' she said. 'I'm working.'

'So am I. I might not be playing a tournament right now but the tennis season is so long, practically all year round.' He took a sip of the water. 'Even when I'm not competing the training is still full-on.

'I see.'

'There *are* other vices that don't affect my game.'

At least in his opinion they didn't affect it. His coach and sponsors might not agree.

She looked him in the eye, a flash of something there that he couldn't fathom. As if she was sizing him up.

'You mean groupies?' she said loudly, blue eyes narrowing.

She was bold, he had to hand it to her. Then again, she'd probably read the gutter press this week, along with the rest of the world.

'Groupie is such an ugly word,' he said. 'Insulting somehow. Makes it sound like I take advantage of people and I can understand that because of the way the papers portray it, but that's just not the way it is. I don't have time for proper full-on relationships and I meet plenty of girls who feel exactly the same way as me. I'm single. I'm not doing anything wrong.' He held her gaze steadily, waiting to gauge her reaction. 'There's a lot to be said for uncomplicated one-off flings,' he said. 'As long as both people know what they're doing, know where they stand, I just don't see what's wrong with it.'

She gave a dismissive whatever-you-say shrug.

Uncomplicated. When did she do anything in her life that was that?

'What about you?' he said. 'Who was it?'

'What do you mean?'

'On the phone. Who was it? Husband? Boyfriend?'

'My mother,' she said shortly. God that made her sound like some saddo spinster who still lived at home with her parents. Whereas it was in fact the other way round. Her mother was the one sponging off her.

He didn't look particularly judgemental. Maybe he had an insane parent tucked away somewhere too. Then again, who was she kidding? He was bound to have rich parents who'd poured money into his tennis career. She pictured him as a toddler wielding a racquet that was bigger than he was and a small twist of envy jabbed at her ribs. He would have had all the opportunities that a supportive family could give you. There was the difference between them. He had the world at his feet and she was one step away from the gutter.

'Makes sense. You need a relative to invoke a tantrum that size.'

'It was NOT some tantrum. I'm twenty four, not four. It was anger. Pure, white hot, tear-her-head-from-her-shoulders anger.'

He pulled a face.

'Wow. Remind me not to get on the wrong side of you.'

She managed a smile and groped for a potted explanation before he could pigeon-hole her as scary freak.

'She's cleaned out my savings account and disappeared across the world on some ridiculous mid-life crisis trip.' She pointed her pen at him. 'The States. Your neck of the woods. I was trying to talk her down but she was already at the airport, tickets in hand, and nothing was going to stop her.' She shrugged. 'I'm normally a pretty level-headed person, I just lost it, that's all. I'd been saving for years.'

Exasperation twisted her stomach again, this time with a sense of defeat that made her want to crash her head down on the coffee table next to the sofa. Her mother would be airborne now, winging her way across the Atlantic, and Layla might just as well have withdrawn her savings from the bank and chucked them in the bin for all the likelihood she had of ever seeing them again.

'For what?'

She shrugged.

'A place of my own.'

The chances of achieving that dream now were non-existent, certainly for the next few years. For some reason saying it out loud invoked a surge of despair that made her throat feel suddenly tight and achy. She swallowed like mad and bit her lower lip, hard to distract herself. She was absolutely *not* going to lose it in front of a stranger. Especially a stranger who had everything. He probably had half a dozen places of his own on various different continents.

'Just you and your mom then?' he said. 'Any other relatives? Married, single, other?'

The only good thing about that question was that it distracted her from her misery. Was he actually sizing her up as a prospect? Good grief, was this how he operated – checking out his prey in a few quick sentences to see if they had strings attached or not? He was looking at her in a boldly appraising way that made her stomach feel like melty marshmallow, as if he could see right inside her. She took a calming sip of her orange juice.

'Single,' she said.

He continued to look at her expectantly. She would have loved to be the kind of confident person who felt no need to fill deliberate pauses in conversations, but the age-old need to be liked and respected had total control when it came to holding her tongue.

'I don't have time for relationships,' she heard herself elaborating. He was nodding encouragement. 'I've been trying to get on at work, save some money up for a flat.' A rueful laugh bubbled out of her. 'Not that I've actually got any savings anymore. And this job isn't exactly nine-to-five. Socialising takes a bit of a back seat.'

'Ah the job again,' he said, sitting back a little on the sofa. 'So there's really no limit to any request I might make?'

A calming wave of relief that the conversation was back on a professional footing made her breathe easier.

'Nope,' she said, giving him an enthusiastic smile. 'No limit. We had an actress not long ago who took a whole floor for her entourage and had every room repainted candy pink. Or on a lesser scale, scented candles in the room are a biggie. Or banks of flowers on every surface. No request too great, too off-the-wall, too diva...'

She trailed away with the PR spiel as he continued to watch her, his gaze holding hers absolutely steady, the expression on his face like the cat who was about to steal the cream.

'And what about more…*personal* requests.'

His eyes creased at the corners, the lopsided smile that had melted the hearts of the nation's women played at his lips.

Her heart began thundering as if she'd just taken the four-storey hotel stairwell two at a time. He was coming onto her. Wasn't he? Why on earth would someone like him look twice at someone like her? If it had been anyone else self-doubt might have won the day and she would have dismissed the idea out of hand, but then this *was* Matt Stanton. The track record of his personal life spoke for itself, he'd bedded more women than she'd had hot coffees.

She'd been a fan of his for years. It wasn't just his skill and grace on the tennis court, it was the same thing that afflicted the rest of the female species. Women fell at his feet, at which point he picked them up, had the time of his life and then dropped them again just as abruptly. Most infuriating of all, that bachelor-playboy persona seemed to make him all the more desirable.

None of them seemed to mind. Even the kiss n' tell stories were, when you got right down to it, ultimately complimentary, this morning's offering a perfect case in point. She thought back to the morning tabloids – **My hot aeroplane encounter with Mile-High Matt** splashed across the front pages with accompanying grainy mobile phone pic of his naked and very muscular butt.

'If you're saying what I think you're saying, I'm *not* a groupie,' she heard herself say, thinking of her mother's insane mission to follow a has-been rock group to another continent. No way was she being categorised alongside that.

Rock stars, tennis stars, it was all interchangeable. What it amounted to was basking in the fringes of someone else's celebrity, as if the excitement in their lives would somehow rub off on your own supermarket-shopping nine-to-five-daily-grind existence.

'I don't care if you are or not,' he said. 'The popular press might have it down differently but whether you believe it or not that's not the single characteristic I look for in a woman.'

'But you've known me for five minutes,' she protested.

He shrugged.

'Why does that have to be a negative? If you think about it for a moment you'll see it opens up a world of possibility. There's no background hangups to get past, no baggage to talk over and get in the way, no irritating friends and family members to get along with. No hoops to jump through. Just you and me. This room. And whatever we want it to be.'

He leaned forward, reached a tentative hand out and stroked a finger gently across her cheek, the lightest of touches which sent sparks of heat flying through her.

OMG Matt Stanton just touched my cheek!

This was exactly the kind of situation her mother had chased since before Layla was born, and now it had simply presented itself to her as if by magic. An unexpected surge of righteous in-your-face defiance caught her by surprise. Dull and boring, was she? Life passing her by? The hottest man in world tennis had just propositioned her without needing so much as a *hint* of encouragement. She wasn't even dressed up for Pete's sake, she was wearing the usual hideous charcoal grey hotel uniform, name badge pinned to her lapel, happy-to-help smile pasted on her face. Not a leather bustier in sight.

Hot on the heels of the defiance came an idea that was so wildly outside her remit that it made her feel dizzy and she held her glass of orange juice tightly in both hands and took a calming sip of it to steady herself.

Her life as it stood at this moment in time wasn't exactly scaling the dizzy heights of success, was it? Her mother's parting words gnawed at her pride and self-belief deep down on a base level. Maybe she could have brushed them off if she was holding down some high-flying job and living an upwardly mobile life in a flat of her own, but the fact was, she wasn't even close. However hard she might try to crush it, there was a tiny bit of her that wondered whether her mother might actually have a point when it came to life. What exactly had twenty four years of striving for respectability got her?

It had been no picnic staking a claim for common sense and normality in the middle of the chaotic one-crazy-minute-at-a-time lifestyle of her mother. Since reaching adulthood the desire for a place of her own had reached dizzying heights, the need for proper roots and security driving her on to work ever longer hours.

And just where exactly had it got her?

For the first time she could remember, looking into the melting brown eyes full of suggestion, with the day becoming crazier by the minute, she questioned her own judgement and beliefs.

Thanks to her mother she was as far away from saving a deposit up as ever. She had a tiny rented studio with sparse shared facilities and a job that left hardly any surplus at the end of the month for savings. The endless grind of that wore her down. Her friend Lucy, one of the many waitressing staff, had a buzzing social life which she lived to the full, never knowing or caring what the next moment might bring. Layla rarely had time or funds for any of that.

Why not do something outside her comfort zone for once? Her comfort zone hadn't exactly delivered much in the way of comfort so far. The thought of doing something reckless and impulsive felt suddenly very exciting, as if she would be stepping outside her own nightmare of a life into a glamorous unpredictable world where anything could happen. For a moment there she actually weakened.

And then reality bit her squarely on the arse.

What was she *doing*? Was this the kind of thought that travelled around her mother's brain on a loop? She was under no illusions about how exciting and interesting she was when put up against the draw of fame and fortune, her mother had spent her whole life illustrating that very point. She had no truck with fame or celebrities and was she really about to be seduced by the very thing she'd spent her whole life abhorring?

She grimly ignored the delicious flip flops going on in her stomach as he smiled at her and forced herself to put her glass down on the table. She stood up, put a few paces between them and swallowed hard to channel calm and squash the surge of you're-not-turning-him-down-are-you disappointment that had begun to rise in her stomach to replace the butterflies. He didn't get up, simply lounged back on the sofa looking up at her in amusement, a smile still playing about his lips. He was utterly, breathtakingly gorgeous. But the fact that she owned a calendar depicting him in a different bare-torsoed pose for each month of the year had no place whatsoever in this debate.

'I need to check on a few things downstairs,' she said, leaning in to grab her clipboard from the table and backing away at speed. 'If you need anything, call the number for Guest Services. It's attached to the phone.'

She heard his relaxed laugh as she headed for the door.

'I'll do that,' he called after her.

***

'I've just been hit on by Matt Stanton,' Layla said, scratching her head. 'At least I think I have.'

Now she was out of the gorgeous luxury of the Kerry Suite and back down here in the reality check that was the sparse staff quarters of the hotel, she began to question her own perception. Why the hell would Matt Stanton hit on her? He could have anyone he chose.

Her friend Lucy's eyebrows met in a frown and she quit making coffee to give Layla her full attention.

'You've *what*?'

Layla glanced quickly around her and lowered her voice to an uncertain whisper.

'I think I've just been hit on by Matt Stanton,' she repeated.

Lucy squealed mad laughter.

'You kill me! Course you have! And I'm marrying George Clooney this weekend. He's popping over to pick me up in his private jet.'

There was a brief stab of indignant offense because she was clearly so undesirable that the idea of Matt Stanton giving her a second glance was a joke.

'He's staying in the Kerry Suite on the top floor,' Layla said. 'It's all been hushed up because he's having trouble with the press and he needed a last-minute bolthole to get away from all the fuss.'

Layla waited patiently until the laughter petered out and an expression of incredulity replaced it.

'*The* Matt Stanton? The tennis playboy with the abs to die for? He's staying here? Omigod I'm such a fan.' She stared into space, her mind obviously working overtime. 'I wonder if I can get a transfer from waiting tables into room service for the week. You know, in case he orders some food in, or champagne. Some of those celebs are like that you know, don't like slumming it in the public restaurant with the rest of us.'

Oh for Pete's sake.

'He said he doesn't usually drink champagne,' Layla said. 'He had mineral water and I had orange juice.'

'You had a *drink* with him?'

Did she have to sound so amazed by that fact?

'Yes. And he was going on about personal requests.'

Lucy rolled her eyes enviously at the ceiling.

'I am soooo jealous! So when are you going to follow it up? You know...' she winked at Layla '...make your next move?'

She spoke as if it was perfectly natural to throw yourself at a celebrity if he happened to wander into your path.

'I'm not. Of course I'm not. It's more than my job's worth.'

Although actually her job wasn't worth an awful lot right now, was it? She was busting a gut all hours and stuck in dismal rental accommodation for the foreseeable future. Disappointment suddenly seemed to be mixing with something else in her churning stomach. Something that felt an awful lot like regret.

'It's not more than mine's worth,' Lucy said, grinning.

'So you wouldn't have any scruples about having a fling with

Matt Stanton then, even though he has the worst reputation ever for womanising. It would never lead to anything. He's on the front of the tabloids with a different girl every week. Wouldn't that bother you?'

Lucy shrugged and stirred a spoonful of sugar into her coffee mug.

'Why would it? It would just be a quickie and it would actually be one to remember for once. Why make it such a big deal? Imagine having a fling with Matt Stanton.' She sighed wistfully. 'He's absolutely gorgeous. And anyway everyone has ill-conceived flings in their past. One-night-stands that you wish you'd never done. Holiday romances that you shag on the beach and then never see again.'

'I don't,' Layla said.

'Yeah well, you're not like the rest of us are you?' She pointed at Layla with her teaspoon. 'You're…you know…*sensible*.'

She apparently tried to put a positive spin on that statement by adding a consoling smile, but it had no effect whatsoever.

When you got right down to it that was just another way of calling her *boring*. And she'd heard that once too often today.

'Anyway,' Lucy picked up her coffee mug and headed off towards the kitchens. 'He was probably only messing about anyway. I mean, come on, he could have anyone he wanted, right?'

Tact was certainly not Lucy's strong point. For some reason that parting comment grated hideously, the clear implication being that she had to be mistaken. Sensible, boring and now deluded that he could even have been interested in her at all. An inner defiance surfaced that might have been there all along, but more likely came from that final straw of a dismissive comment on the back of the crappy day from hell she'd had so far.

Five minutes later and she was stalking back down the top floor passageway at top speed, heart thundering loud enough in her ears to drown out the tired old voice in her head that had kept her on the straight and narrow all these years.

He opened the door of the suite on her first knock and she burst into the room, riding the wave of defiant impulsiveness and crappy-day-from-hellness. The feeling it gave her turned out to be surprisingly liberating. Suddenly, unfettered by her endless drive for respect and normality, anything felt possible. She caught the briefest glimpse of his eyes widening in surprise as before she could change her mind, she stood on her tiptoes, curled one arm around his neck and planted a kiss squarely on his mouth.

CHAPTER THREE

Too stunned to do anything but stand there, he froze until she pulled away, breathing hard. The look in her wide eyes was a mixture of shock and exhilaration.

It wasn't often that women surprised him. He'd been faintly amused by her determination to give him the brush-off. It all added to the fun, right? He certainly hadn't expected Miss Straight-Down-The-Line to do a u-turn all by herself, and had in fact been idling away the half hour since she'd left the suite considering his own next move. Yet apparently his charm had a presence of its own, continuing to work even when he wasn't present. And now that she had made that u-turn, it would be rude not to respond, right?

Initially caught off-guard, he quickly reclaimed control of the situation. He looked down into the china blue eyes and took in her short, quick breaths and the expression on her face of nervous excitement. Really, she was so cute. He took his time to savour the triumph as he slid his hands into her far-too-tidy hair and angled her jaw perfectly with a stroke of his thumbs. Slowly now, his pace not hers, he kissed her.

The touch of his lips and the slide of his hand around her waist sent delicious sparks of heat flying down her spine. Rationality almost made a last-minute comeback. One little move and she could still undo this madness, she could have the status of the girl who'd knocked back Matt Stanton, maybe that could have its own special kudos. She could go right on back to the daily grind, the work-hard-and-get-nowhere treadmill that she'd been on for years.

Maybe on a normal day rationality might have stood a chance. But today second thoughts didn't seem to have an awful lot going for them. After the day she'd had the thought of behaving badly and tasting life seemed like the best idea she'd had in years. Why not find out exactly what it was she was supposed to be missing out on. At least then she could argue her point with her nutty mother from a position of knowledge. And let's face it, behaving well for the last twenty four years hadn't really yielded any results, had it?

She shoved away the voice of reason and let herself melt against him. There was no grabbing, no fast moves, he was making it clear that every step of this was something to relish, not a crazy rush. Just one single connection, his lips against hers, slowly intensified by his hand as he slipped it into her hair to cradle the nape of her neck. Tingling heat spiralled through her body to pool in an intense flutter between her legs.

And all the while the neon sign flashed in her mind.

Matt Stanton is KISSING YOU! You have his calendar hanging downstairs in your locker!

He took her lower lip between his own and sucked gently, caressing her lips apart with his tongue. Her hands crept around his neck, wanting more of that delicious connection, and excitement rose inside her like a crowd of butterflies, masking reality, buffering out the inhibiting real world of choices and consequences.

Losing herself.

She let her hands slide up his chest and knitted fingers behind his neck. His shoulders were gorgeous. The *breadth* of them. The solidity. And the strength in his arms and hands, the latent power beneath his lightness of touch. You could feel protected from anything wrapped in arms like those.

This was the ultimate in shallow encounters and that in itself felt suddenly exciting. Work was forgotten. Responsibility was forgotten. This was about proving a point – to her mother, damn right, but more importantly to herself. Payback time and damn the consequences. This moment was hers, she could take what pleasure she wanted from it. No complications. That thought was somehow freeing and intoxicating and she tugged at his polo shirt, pulled it free from his jeans, wanting to explore. He slid a hand around her waist and tugged her further into the room kissing her as he went, stopping briefly to pull the shirt over his head and throw it to the floor. Free now to touch him, she slid curious hands slowly up his tanned chest to his huge shoulders. Not a scrap of fat laced his body. Desire burned hotly through her at the feel of taut skin sheathing hard muscle.

If she'd imagined this scene it wouldn't have been like this. It would have been super-fast, detached. Wasn't that the way these celebrity types worked? Get it on, get their rocks off, move on. In her mind it would have involved champagne, swigged perhaps from one of his tennis cups. Loud music. Hangers-on in the main suite while he took her in the bedroom. Alcohol aplenty.

Not water and orange juice and just the two of them.

His hands were inside her jacket, easing it off her shoulders. She shrugged her way out of it and he threw it aside, his fingers returning to find the buttons of her blouse and pull it away. He traced a soft line of stomach-melting kisses along her shoulder blade while his fingers slid around her back to her bra hook. Too late she remembered that it was a hideous old one in greying manky t-shirt fabric and she grabbed his face with both hands and kissed him hard to stop him seeing it. The second it was loose she snagged it away from him and threw it somewhere behind her. Shyness kicked briefly back in when he tugged at her skirt until it fell to her feet, and then delicious sensation was rushing her mind and crushing everything in its way. His hands had slipped back upwards to find her breasts, cupping them in his palms, lightly pinching the nipples between his fingers until she gasped against his mouth, and she felt his lips move against hers in a smile of satisfaction at her response. The sensation was so intense she felt weak with it, thought vaguely that her legs might give way, and then his hand eased beneath her and he picked her up as if she weighed nothing and walked her to the dark wood table across the room.

He set her down on the table top, and slowly eased her down until its cool glossy surface was hard beneath her back. She gazed up at the high ceiling, too shy to look him in the face as he trailed his fingers down slowly over her breasts, lower now across her stomach, and then finding the thin fabric of her panties, easing them down and away. Then his fingers were teasing between her legs, delicate fluttering strokes giving a hint of what was to follow. She felt his eyes on her, watching her laid bare in front of him, and when curiosity finally made her look she found herself unable to tear her eyes away from his steady gaze as he greedily took in her every reaction to his touch. Fingertips played at her entrance, teasing her with a little pleasure until she squirmed against him, then he removed his hand and made her wait for more. Over and over he aroused her further, then stopped until she found herself writhing against his hand, clutching the hard sides of the table, wanting more, aching for him to fill that emptiness, unable to think of anything else.

He leaned forward to kiss her and she clutched at him hungrily, shocked by the way her desire crushed everything in its path. Yet still as he began to move slowly lower she reached out and tangled her hand in his hair, the intimacy of what he intended beyond what she'd expected, beyond what she'd done before.

'Wait…' she said.

He caught her hand in his, twining his fingers into hers, kissing her fingertips.

'Trust me,' he said gently, smiling encouragement at her.

A pause as she let his reassurance take hold, physical desire winning out over shyness, then she lay slowly back inch by inch, trying to relax, letting her eyes flutter shut.

She'd expected him to be skilled. For goodness sake, the man's sexual prowess was documented on gossip websites and in the popular press. She hadn't expected him to take such delight in her own satisfaction. When had she last had sex? Not since she'd moved to London two years ago, landing her first hotel job through a friend.

And when had she ever had sex like this? Shameless, no-holds-barred delicious out-of-character sex with someone who was so physically fit and gorgeous that she wanted to keep her eyes open all the time to check he was real? Never.

He traced tiny soft kisses down the hollow of her stomach, his tongue tracing her navel, and then she tensed in anticipation as she felt his breath, hot against the very core of her. She felt a single caressing stroke of his tongue parting her and then she was crying out at the ceiling as he sucked lightly at the sensitive nub beneath. The sensation drove out all thoughts of anything else and she reached down to sink shaky fingers into his hair. Holding her hard against his mouth he slid two fingers smoothly inside her, and in response to her soft moan added another, thrusting now with expert rhythm while she raised her hips from the table, desperate for every drop of pleasure he offered, inhibitions dissolving in such sweet ecstasy that she forgot where she was, forgot about shyness or anger and proving a point, forgot everything but that delicious connection with him.

As her breath slowly evened she became aware again of the hard surface beneath her, the room. As he softly kissed her inner thighs she leaned up on her elbows, pushed herself to sit up and tugged him up towards her, curling her arms around his neck. His mouth found hers again and he kissed her hungrily as she ran her hands over his drum-tight torso and down his body to find his erection, delighting in his sharp intake of breath when she ran her fingertips over its velvety length. She began to stroke, found a natural rhythm and kept going until he let out a gutteral moan and took her hand in his.

Moving urgently now, his hand flat against her stomach, he pulled her against him and turned her over, her feet sinking into the deep pile rug, her breasts pressed flat against the cold wood table top. A moment's pause as he found a condom and then she felt him behind her, his breath against her back as he traced kisses down her spine. She heard herself moan with anticipation as he circled the core of her with his rigid erection and then in one smooth movement he thrust inside her to the hilt. She gasped as he took her, each stroke long and hard, filling her completely, his hand sliding beneath her to cup her breast, her nipple lightly pinched in his thumb and forefinger. As he pushed her over the edge of her climax her cries misted the gloss of the table top beneath her, and he gasped his own pleasure against her bare shoulder as he finally let himself lose control.

*****

She lay against his shoulder, and the tension in her neck and back was pretty soon going to start making her jaw ache. At some point in the last hour they'd made it to the pair of sofas and now the rough silk of the crushed velvet lay against her bare skin. Her mind raced and her heart kept pace with it, because now that there was no delicious sex to distract her, all that was left to contemplate was the horror of what she'd done. Twenty-odd years ago, she could have been her mother.

And after a lifetime of contempt for *that* kind of behaviour had she really just gone and done this?

His fingers stroked her upper arm in a rhythmic motion. Gentle. Affectionate even. She hadn't expected that to be a part of his post-shag repertoire, hadn't expected him to want to, well, *lie with her*. She'd expected him to be up and dressed and sending her on her way with a signed photo the second he'd got what he wanted.

'I'll be right back,' he said, dropping a kiss on her bare shoulder.

Then again, there was still time.

He gently disentangled her from his arms and disappeared across the suite in the direction of the bathroom. The second he was out of sight she scrambled to her feet. Her uniform lay strewn in haphazard blobs around the room. Her knickers had somehow made it an astonishing distance across the room to the window sill. His skill at lobbing clearly wasn't limited to tennis balls. She dashed around the room, picking up her blouse and skirt and holding them bunched against her chest and she'd mercifully just climbed into her knickers when he emerged from the bathroom.

He stared at her lurking by the window with a bemused expression on his face. Her mind, clearly still attuned on some unconscious level to the utter gorgeousness of him, zeroed in on the fact that he was wearing petrol blue shorts and nothing else. His dark hair was dishevelled. She could see the eagle tattoo on the hard curve of his tanned bicep.

She cut her eyes away with a massive effort. She glanced around madly for her bra, couldn't see it and made an attempt to put her shirt on without flashing him.

'You're going?' he said, stating the obvious.

She jabbed buttons through holes on the blouse. As long as she looked vaguely decent she could tuck herself in and straighten herself out in the Ladies Room on the way down to the lobby. Every extra moment spent in here was a moment too long.

'I'm getting back to work,' she said.

'There's no need for that.' A playful grin lit his face.

'There's every need,' she said. 'I could get the sack for this!'

She shoved her hands into the sleeves of her jacket and looked around the room for her shoes.

He crossed the room and touched her arm gently.

'No one's getting the sack,' he said. 'You're with me. Any problems, I'll have them smoothed out.'

She spotted one of her shoes underneath the opposite sofa and scrambled to her knees to hook it out.

'You're not living in the real world,' she said, balancing on one leg to put it on and wobbling madly. She wondered briefly how long this weak-at-the-knees effect was likely to carry on. 'Do you actually think your name counts for anything when it comes to my job? You might be able to career through life doing whatever the hell you please because you've got a little bit of kudos but your get-out-of-jail-free card won't work on my bosses. Trust me.'

'Girls aren't normally this eager to run out on me,' he said. 'Did I do something wrong?'

'Nope,' she said, finding the other shoe near the fireplace and putting it on. She was dressed enough to make an exit now. 'That would be me. It's all been a HUGE mistake. So if you could maybe forget it ever happened, I'll do the same.'

'You want to forget that this...' his eyes darted towards the glossy dining table and then met hers with a raise of the eyebrows that made her cheeks burn at what they'd just done there '...that *this* ever happened?'

God he had an ego to match the size of his manhood. This was clearly the part where as a normal groupie she would be meant to fawn over him and fan his massive ego until he got bored, at which point he would scout around for his next conquest and she would fade into the background, perhaps with just a parting whisper of gratitude as she went. No way was she giving that a chance to happen. She'd slept with him now, there was no going back and changing that, but it didn't mean she had to carry on with the madness now it was done.

'Absolutely,' she said, looking him straight in the eye and smoothing her hair back from her face with both hands. She could just imagine what a fright it must look and she daren't even hazard a guess at how her mascara had stood up to the experience. 'I don't want you to autograph my knickers, I'm not going to steal any of your belongings as a trophy and I'm sorry to disappoint you but I am actually going to shower later and wash off all your kisses.'

He was staring at her, a look of amusement on his face, not remotely fazed. He'd made no attempt to obstruct her, had simply watched her dashing around the room and speed dressing with a smile playing about his lips.

***

Bit of a curved ball this.

He had just worked out how to operate the controls on the hot tub, plans already forming in his head for a slow and languorous second-round laced with bubbles and waterjets, and she was on her way out of the door. He'd been ready to settle into an all-night experience, seeing how many more of her inhibitions he could erase.

The shoulder-length blonde hair was no longer sleek and groomed. Instead it flicked out in haphazard waves which gave away exactly what she'd just been doing. And just looking at her like that, with her sensible make-up a bit smudgy now around her blue eyes, fired him right back up.

Girls running out on him was uncharted territory. Where was the feverish writing down of phone numbers, the begging for assurances that yes, he would call (which in the event meant no, he certainly wouldn't)? Where were the requests to have photos taken with him for sharing on Facebook? And more to the point, when had he ever post-sex had a girl ask *him* to forget about it and treat it as if it had never happened?

That was his remit, wasn't it? Maybe he was losing his touch. Had the last hour or so not been the most glorious experience? The way she'd slowly given up her shyness, shed inhibitions, put her trust in him and worked with him to push things to heights so dizzy he was actually stunned? She'd never had sex like that before, he knew it because she'd given it away with her hesitation, and that she'd trusted him enough to go with her instincts touched him on a visceral level that didn't usually come into play.

She was heading for the door now, clothes in disarray, jacket slung over one arm. He saw her dart to one side as she spotted

30

her bra hanging over a side table and grabbed at it.

'What if I need some arrangements making?' he called after her. 'Errands running…car…room service…?'

'There's a number attached to the phone,' she said.

'And will I get you?'

She paused at the door and turned back.

'I'm one of a team,' she said. The look on her face told him that the real answer was a resounding 'no'. Exasperation made him roll his eyes. She was a mass of infuriating contradictions. How could someone who'd given their everything to him in the last hour or so now be backtracking so fast he could barely keep up?

She held the door open for a split second while she took a quick glance each way down the corridor, and then she slipped through the gap and was gone. The door clicked softly shut behind her.

CHAPTER FOUR

'What the hell's the matter with you?'

When she looked up she saw Lucy staring at her from the staff room doorway and perhaps sitting with her head in her hands wasn't the best way to deflect attention and pretend everything was normal. It did, however, seem to help calm her racing brain.

'I've become my mother,' she said.

Lucy pulled a puzzled face.

'You mean you're off round the world to follow some boy band? Or are you planning on doing the festival season next year, sleeping in a tent and drinking mead?' Her voice was jokey. Because of course the idea of Layla Jones doing something like that was so out of character that it really was a joke.

'For Pete's sake, you're missing the point!' she wailed. 'I've *slept* with him.'

This time it seemed to penetrate. Lucy's mouth fell open.

'Him? You don't mean Matt Stanton?'

Disbelief dominated her expression and Layla felt the teeniest hint of offense. Was it really THAT hard to believe?

'Yes. After we talked before, I went up to check the suite, see if there was anything he needed.' How easily *that* lie tripped off her tongue, as if she was trying to convince herself as much as Lucy that it really hadn't been quite that premeditated. 'And my head was spinning with all that stuff you said about being boring and never acting on impulse…' she threw up her hands '…one thing led to another.' She clapped both hands over her eyes. 'What have I done?'

'Was he good?'

The bottom fell out of her stomach just from thinking about it. *Good* really didn't have a hope in hell of covering it. And the fact that deep down there was a part of her that was exhilarated by what she'd done only added to her horror at herself. In a single afternoon, she'd betrayed every single belief she'd lived by for the last twenty-odd years. She looked between her fingers at Lucy.

'That's totally irrelevant.'

'Actually, it isn't. There's a world of distance between a one-night-stand that's pants and one that's good.'

'Technically it's not even a one-night-stand. More a couple-of-hours-stand. If there is such a thing.'

'Good for you.'

'Good? How can it be good? I could be sacked on the spot.'

'Why? Did you get caught?'

'No, but—'

'Did you take precautions?'

'Of course I did! I'm not a total idiot.'

Lucy shrugged.

'Then don't worry about it. Layla, you are not the first woman in the world to have a one-off quickie. This isn't the Dark Ages. It really is not such a big deal.' She pulled out her mobile phone and began to casually check her texts, clearly so unfazed by the revelation that she was bored with it already. 'Chill out, will you,' she added.

Layla stared at her.

'I'm a slut.'

'You're a woman who makes her own choices.' Lucy said, then returned to the only thing about the situation that really seemed to be of interest. 'So was he?'

'What?'

'Good?'

Oh for crying out loud.

***

It never happened.

She'd repeated that mantra over and over throughout the restless, sleep-deprived night in the hope that soon her brain might actually start to believe it. She regretted telling Lucy about it now. It became a whole lot harder to deny something to yourself once you'd let someone else in on it.

The following morning she took deliberately shallow, calming breaths as she crossed the marble floor of the lobby to the reception desk to check for messages. It was perfectly simple. *Business as usual* was the approach here. All she needed to do was get through his stay here without coming into contact with him. That and avoid watching tennis on TV ever again so she wouldn't see him and be reminded of the most insane decision she'd ever made.

She absently picked up a tabloid newspaper left on one of the lobby tables as she passed and glanced casually at its front cover, a colour photo depicting Matt Stanton and his perfect abs frolicking in the surf at some swanky beach resort with a stunning blonde model. Shallow breaths turned into hyperventilation.

Better add avoiding the papers into that game plan.

'Ah there you are, thought you'd gone AWOL, been looking for you for the last half hour.'

She turned, heart plummeting, to see the hotel manager with his usual overbearing presence and the sharp eyes in the jowly face that always made her feel like he was ready to pounce if she put a foot wrong. She tried desperately to channel cool, calm professionalism when she was certain her guilty conscience would show on her face.

'Is there a problem?' she asked, forcing a bright smile and

following his grey-suited bulk into the office behind the marble counter. He closed the door behind them.

'Our *special guest*, Kerry Suite,' he began and her stomach fell through the floor. 'Called down to discuss what Guest Services offer.'

Oh bloody hell he's made a complaint.

Cold shock thumped through her veins as the ramifications of this pelted through her head. Dismissal on the spot, that's what this was. She'd never get a reference after this. She'd never be able to keep up the rent and she had zero savings to carry her through while she tried to pin down another job. This was it, the perfect end to the craziest day, the final coup de grace.

She was about to get the sack for shagging a celebrity guest.

The hideous irony of it twisted her stomach. She of all people should have known better. Basking in the fringes of celebrity meant you could be soaking up the glamour one minute and kicked back into the gutter the next.

'I can explain,' she said, wondering how the hell she possibly could.

'Wants to use one of our staff exclusively for the week,' he spoke loudly over her. 'PA duties, a few errands, organising, that kind of thing. Apparently he doesn't want a butler, wants to limit the number of staff he comes into contact with, something about keeping a low profile.' His face screamed disapproval. 'He's never out of the press, obviously must be wanting to take a break. Anyway,' he nodded at her, 'asked for you by name.'

He what?

The brief relief at the revelation that he hadn't actually reported her and she wasn't about to be handed her P45 was trampled by her heart, which kicked into action with full-on sweaty-palmed thundering. He wanted to *use her exclusively* for the week? What the hell did that mean? Did he really need someone to run errands and make his travel arrangements, or did *using her exclusively* mean something altogether different? The image of his muscular frame looming over her as she lay on the Kerry Suite dining table flashed unbidden into her mind. She felt suddenly light headed and sank into the chair beside the desk before she could fold onto the thick pile carpet.

'I'm not sure I'm the best choice,' she said weakly. 'Guest Services is madly busy, constant phone calls and requests from guests and the boss is off sick. Wouldn't one of the concierge team be a better bet?'

Possibly the skinny male one with the laugh like a drain. He'd be perfectly safe.

A decisive shake of the head.

'Job's yours, already agreed. Can't possibly spare a concierge, short staffed there as it is. And between you and me, this could be an excellent move for you.'

He tapped the side of his nose in an I-know-something-you-don't-know gesture. She stared at him. What the hell did that mean? He leaned across the desk and lowered his voice.

'You mentioned Margery is on sick leave? Worse than expected apparently - she's just handed her notice in.'

Her boss Margery, Guest Services Manager, who ran the team like a tyrant and who definitely would NOT condone an ill-judged fling with a guest.

'The job will be advertised internally first. You've been with us for a couple of years, you've done all the courses, proved yourself, so pull this one-to-one service off for the week and you could have the promotion in the bag. This kind of celebrity guest is exactly what the place needs to up the hotel's profile and get us playing with the big boys. So get yourself up to the Kerry Suite and keep that guest happy. Everyone's a winner.'

***

Everyone was most definitely NOT a winner.

The manager's job could be her saving grace. Finally she could be making enough money to start moving forwards instead of madly paddling just to keep her head above water. She could save up a new deposit, she'd be a better prospect for a mortgage. A proper secure future with a bit of certainty about it for a change. But all she needed to do to make it happen was not stuff this up. Plans to avoid Matt Stanton like the plague for the week went out of the window and she tried desperately to come up with some kind of rational approach as the lift took her smoothly up to the top floor.

Maybe he really did just need a temporary assistant for the week to handle his admin while he stayed here. It wasn't exactly unusual for the hotel to allow guests to utilise their staff when required. If you were prepared to paint a whole floor candy pink giving up one of your staff instead of calling in a temp from an agency was really a no-brainer.

Except that he'd asked for her by name. And surely that could only mean one thing: the kind of personal services he was looking for had nothing to do with making travel arrangements and doing a few secretarial jobs.

There was nothing else for it, she would just have to convince Matt Stanton that she wasn't up for a week-long stint as his plaything. She'd already made it clear that what had happened between them was a mistake, all she needed to do was stick to that line.

If she could pull it off.

She kept her eyes fixed on the panel of lift buttons instead of checking her reflection in its mirrored wall as she usually did, just to prove to herself that she definitely did not give a toss what Matt Stanton thought of her appearance. This would be about providing a professional service. Nothing more. And if she could just keep things on that kind of detached level her life might look a whole lot more optimistic in a week's time.

And it would be a whole lot easier if her stupid heart stopped skipping a beat every time she thought of him.

'Good of you to knock,' he said as he opened the door. He was wearing jeans and a sea green shirt that did nothing to hide the broad muscular shoulders, sleeves pushed up to the elbows to reveal his strong tanned forearms. His hair was softly tousled and his brown eyes creased lightly at the corners as he leaned against the jamb and smiled his melt-your-stomach smile. Her heart, clearly not up to speed on the absolute requirement for professionalism here, did a soft little skip in her chest.

Warmth rose in her cheeks as she crossed the room to stand by the rolltop desk in the corner and turned to face him. She deliberately averted her eyes from the glossy dining table in her peripheral vision. It was hard enough to stop her mind from providing constant reruns of what had gone on over there, without actually *looking* at the scene. She turned to him, spiral notebook upraised like a shield in front of her chest, pen poised to take notes.

'Perhaps we can start with a brief outline of the tasks you think you need covering. That will give me an indication of how to adjust my working hours. I've been covering the late shift this last week or two but I can change that around depending on the kind of admin support you're after.'

Admin support. That was good. That sounded officey.

He waved a dismissive hand her way.

'Shouldn't think there's any major need for you to adjust your hours,' he said. 'The whole point of me staying here this week is to refocus on my training and minimise distractions. I have training sessions every morning with an early start so I'm not likely to be in the suite until the afternoon. If you could arrange transport to and from the tennis club I'll be using, that would be great.' He began to count things off on his fingers. 'I also need to keep some control over my nutrition, so I'll provide you with a list of foods I require and those I want to exclude and you can use that to liaise with the kitchen. I assume that won't be a problem?'

She stared at him for a moment, wrongfooted, before her brain clicked into gear and she started making hasty notes as he carried on with a list of run-of-the-mill tasks. The most exciting, and *exciting* was actually a real stretch here, were a list of box set DVD's he wanted tracked down.

Part of her was busy being grateful that she was more than up for the job. There was nothing exactly taxing here. If the list was anything to go by she was going to be bored out of her skull all week. The other part of her was knocked sideways by the revelation that actually, this wasn't about sex, and what the hell was that dragging feeling in her stomach all about? It intensified as the mundane list grew. And she absolutely refused to countenance that it might be disappointment. The last thing she needed or wanted was to pick up where they'd left off the previous evening.

Had he decided on reflection that their encounter simply wasn't worth a second run? It might have been off-the-scale memorable to her but he probably screwed women on dining tables every night of the week. What a stupid arrogant fool she'd been to think he might want to do it more than once with run-of-the-mill sensible and boring Layla Jones.

Turned out he really did want a PA/Admin assistant. Who knew? Apparently sports stars with crazy sex lives still had filing and phone calls to take care of.

'Perhaps you'd like to have some coffee sent up and we can run through the details?'

She made the call while he crossed to the fireplace and sat down on one of the two velvet sofas. She followed him and sat down opposite him. The dining table sat to one side of the suite like the elephant in the room and the faint look of amusement that hung in his eyes told her that he was enjoying that fact, and was watching her awkwardness with interest.

'I'll take meals up in the suite rather than using the restaurant,' he said.

'I guessed that would be the case,' she said, making a note.

'Did you?' he said pointedly, watching her intently as she looked up, her cheeks warming. 'Why is that?'

He was clearly alluding to the grainy pictures of his naked backside that were currently going viral on the internet. Surely he must know his scandalous behaviour of the previous month or so had been trending on Twitter?

'You wouldn't be the first celebrity guest to make that kind of demand,' she said, choosing her words carefully. 'They worry that they'll be hassled for autographs while they're eating their toast and marmalade.'

If she was trying, with her forced professional attitude, to keep the slant of disapproval out of her voice she failed epically. Matt leaned back easily on the sofa and watched her carefully. Unable to sleep the previous evening after her sudden exit curtailed his plans in the most frustrating of ways, and unable to get out of this damned hotel and distract himself at a nightclub or party, he'd instead spent hours being needled by the fact she'd run out on him. It was the contradiction that bothered him. The fact she could have indulged herself so fully in that moment and yet afterward was so desperate to undo it. He'd got his way, letting it slide now would be the sensible thing to do. Yet her lack of interest drove him crazy.

Frankly, he had precious little else to amuse him this week. He needed some respite from the insanity of his training schedule. His team had brought in a new English coach for a different perspective and he was under scrutiny from the moment he arrived at the tennis club until he arrived back here in the late afternoon. And since he'd agreed not to be seen going out, partying or socialising until his sponsors were placated, amusement would instead have to come to him. She fitted the bill perfectly. And arranging to have her as his PA meant she was completely under the radar of the press.

The only problem was that she was looking at him as if she wanted to call security and have him thrown out onto the pavement. Didn't exactly bode well for a few nights of no-strings fun. But still, he liked a challenge, and the result would be so much more satisfying if he had to work for it. Sometimes easy was just too damned easy.

'Why are you so determined to be unimpressed by me?'

he said, holding her gaze deliberately. 'Was yesterday such a disappointment?'

He had the concerned frown on his face of someone whose feelings were on the brink of being hurt. Counterfeit concern surely. She'd read about his exploits in magazines and newspapers for years and from all she knew of him, he didn't usually let concern get in the way of whatever he wanted to do.

Of course it hadn't been disappointing. It had been *mindblowing*, and just at his mention of it her face felt vaguely throbby with heat and she knew she must be looking beetroot-red. She cut her eyes quickly away from his.

'I'd rather not talk about yesterday, if you don't mind,' she said, fiddling with her pen and notebook. 'I thought we agreed it never happened.'

'I just don't understand why you're so regretful of it when you were so enthusiastic at the time. It was fun, wasn't it? We're both adults.' He shrugged. 'No biggie.'

No biggie?

A burst of contempt broke her professional façade before she could stop it. All her intentions to just avoid mentioning it flew out of the window. OK then, if he was determined not to let it lie she could take the opportunity to throw a few truths his way.

'It might be no biggie for *you*,' she snapped. 'Bedding a woman you've just met is clearly the order of the day in your life. I'm not like that.'

He raised questioning eyebrows at her and well he might because yesterday she had been like that. She flapped a hand at him.

'Not usually anyway,' she conceded irritably.

A brief tap on the door signified the coffee arriving and he watched her as she poured them each a cup, concentrating hard on what she was doing instead of looking him in the eye.

'So what was different about yesterday?' he said, not letting her off the hook.

She lifted her cup and saucer and looked across the table at him steadily, a guarded expression in the china blue eyes.

'I had a bit of a crazy day yesterday, I wasn't thinking straight, it just happened,' she said in a rush. Quick dismissal. 'Now it's done I can't take it back however much I might want to, but at least I can draw some kind of line under it.'

'Why would you want to take it back? Why so negative about it? Because from where I was standing it was pretty damned wonderful.'

She tried to ignore the happy skip in her stomach that comment caused.

'Look,' she said, talking slowly and deliberately, making a desperate attempt to close the subject once and for all. 'Let's just say I've had some experience of the way celebrities live and while it might seem glamorous and exciting to lots of the girls you meet, it has absolutely zero pull for me. I like to keep things grounded in the real world. That's the difference between us. So if we could keep things professional between us, that would be good.'

She put her empty coffee cup on the tray and stood up.

'Now, if that's everything, I'll leave you to it while I go and liaise with the kitchen,' she said.

'It isn't everything,' he said, standing up and moving towards her. 'In actual fact it's nothing.' He nodded at the list in her hand. 'All of that stuff is a front. Admin tasks that either don't need doing or that I could easily delegate to a member of my own staff.'

Her heart picked up the pace as he closed the gap between them.

'I was told you wanted one of the hotel staff to work for you this week, in the absence of your own assistant,' she gabbled. 'Are you now saying you don't want that after all?'

'I didn't want one of the hotel staff. I wanted you. And you can carry out all those tasks on the list if you like, but to be perfectly honest the main point of asking you to take on the role was for your company.'

She narrowed eyes at him.

'I'm not talking about sex,' he said, holding his hands up, face the picture of innocence. 'You'll be perfectly safe. I'm just not that great at staying in by myself. I own a share in a nightclub back home, I like to party and I have a full-on social life when I can. Obviously the tennis calendar is pretty in-your-face and I behave differently when I'm playing a tournament, but it's October and things are a bit less crazy right now. I should be making the most of the downtime, but because the press have gone overboard this last month or so my sponsors are demanding I keep a low profile.' She saw a brief flash of defiance cross his face. 'Thing is, I don't really *do* low profile. Staying alone in a hotel room with Pay Per View is not my idea of R and R. So how about you have dinner with me tonight?'

She stared at him. For some reason the way he dismissed sex made her mood, already confused, take a downturn. Not that she wanted to have sex with him again, of course, but it had been kind of flattering to think he wanted to. The idea that he could just take it or leave it made her feel strangely deflated and she was extremely irritated with herself for even caring. Platonic company and a few admin errands? How hard could it be? And with sex resolutely off the agenda she would be perfectly safe.

'Dinner? Here?'

'Yes. Like I said, I'm meant to be staying out of sight. I'm training this afternoon but this evening is completely free. The restaurant's probably not a great idea.'

'And if I say no?'

He burst out laughing.

'You can say whatever you like, Layla.'

The way he used her first name made her stomach give a slow and delicious flip. She bit her lower lip hard to keep her mind on task, even if her body didn't seem to be up to the challenge.

'Haven't you got a friend you can call up? Or family? Why would you want to spend time with me? I'm a total stranger.'

There was a flash in his eyes of something she couldn't quite fathom. Uncertainty was probably the nearest she could get to it.

'I like you,' he said simply. 'You tell it like it is. That's unusual for someone when I first meet them.'

'Don't you think that's down to the kind of people you mix with?' she said. 'Where are your close family and friends? What about a proper home life, proper friends, people who are honest with you? Or do you just have yes-men and hangers-on?'

'It's not like that,' he said.

She looked at the guarded expression on his face, her interest piqued by his evasion.

'What *is* it like then?' she pressed.

He put his head on one side, considering her question.

'It's just the way it works,' he said eventually. 'It's not a deliberate choice who I socialise with, it's just the way things end up. Tennis at this level is incredibly demanding. There isn't a tennis season as such, not in the way there is for football or rugby. It's pretty full on for most of the year.'

'So you're surrounded by adoring fans who don't even know you beyond your media image and your magazine photos.' she said. 'Those things aren't real. That's all just window dressing. Where are your family, where's your proper home life?'

He shrugged.

'I've got a brother and sister but they're based back in Boston, both have got their own lives,' he said. 'My parents are elderly and not particularly sporty so they don't make it to many of my matches. And there's a lot of travel involved. It's kind of hard to keep up family ties when you're on the other side of the world half the time.'

She began moving toward the door.

'It all sounds like a lot of hard work and shallow relationships,' she said. 'I'd have thought your family would watch your every game. If I had a brother like that I'd be so proud I'd go to everything.'

The thought of having family support was intoxicating and she felt a pang of envy that he had siblings. Her own family unit had only ever made her feel alone.

He shrugged.

'Maybe you could see it that way. The rewards are amazing though, beyond anything I could have dreamed of as a kid. And it was never really a conscious decision to let family slip, you just end up so busy that coming into contact with people on a normal level is unheard of. To be perfectly honest when I have downtime I want to have some fun. Sometimes that's a whole lot easier when all it's about is having a good time, the last thing you need is relationship complications.'

She watched him, letting her mind process all that. His life was completely shallow. And shallow was all he wanted from her. Easy, inconsequential company for the week. The familiar old contempt spiked in her stomach. His was exactly the lifestyle her mother had coveted, and practiced, for her entire adult life. The excitement, the glamour, the parties and hangers-on. All the things Layla had learned to loathe as she grew up, the endless distraction of her mother's attention and regard. Oh she might settle down for a month or so, meals would start coming regularly, she would be at home when Layla came in from school, but then festival season would start and she'd disappear to camp in a field with friends while Layla managed as best she could with a succession of friends and relatives, and later when she was old enough, by herself.

'So dinner?' he said again. 'I'll leave you to organise the menu, you've got my nutrition list.'

It was a week. That was all. The promotion hung maddeningly in front of her like a carrot before a starving donkey. She might disagree with his lifestyle and his every principle but what did that matter as long as she got the new position and, more to the point, the pay rise associated with it? She just needed to keep him sweet.

'Fine,' she said.

CHAPTER FIVE

Matt opened the door of the suite that evening on her first knock again and whatever he'd done that day at training, it clearly hadn't pushed him to any physical limit. He looked as fresh as a daisy in his jeans and dark blue shirt, the sleeves casually pushed up. His dark hair was still shower-damp and the light woody notes of his aftershave on warm skin made her stomach go soft. For once she was glad of her grey uniform with the pink piping on the lapels. It felt like armour. Wearing this suit sent out the message that for her, this was about *work*. She didn't look like she was smuggling herself into his room, she was there legitimately. An unnerving flash of clarity followed that thought as it occurred to her that being in his room legitimately might be the whole reason she appealed to him right now. Wasn't his usual type out of bounds in the wake of the recent naked butt scandal?

The suite was cosy, a fire spitting in the grate between the velvet sofas, the thick silk curtains shutting out the endless damp weather. What had happened between them in this room yesterday crackled between them and she fought to block it out.

She could feel his eyes on her as she pushed the room service trolley across the suite and begin moving plates to the table. A delicately presented light meal of jewel-red tuna steak served with mixed salad leaves. Her stomach gave a flip of anticipation as she

46

saw that the food was accompanied by a bottle of champagne on ice.

'Champagne?' she said carefully. 'I didn't order that.'

'I took the liberty,' he said.

His words of the previous evening surfaced in her mind. *Not that I don't drink sometimes, I just choose my moments, make sure they count.* Her heart began to thump so hard she wondered if he might hear it.

She sat down opposite him, picked up her napkin and a fork. The food looked perfect, yet she couldn't have been less interested in it. Every cell in her body felt on edge. She was here at his beck and call, on his say-so, against all her better judgement. Yet there was a hint of danger about going along with this that made her feel more excited and alive than she could remember. She tried her best to crush that feeling by sweeping straight into smalltalk. Nothing like boring life detail to keep an air of detachment. He was hardly going to jump her bones if she could keep the conversation rooted in the day-to-day stuff.

'What's your house like in the States?' she asked.

Matt picked up his knife and fork, glanced up and smiled at her. She didn't smile back. Her expression was detached, polite.

'In Malibu. Beachfront, which is really great. Not that I get much time to spend there. There's so much travel going on that I'm rarely there for more than a few weeks at a time.'

She was pushing her salad around her plate with a fork, not looking at him.

'Must still be nice though. You must be set up for life. And what a dream, to excel at something, find something you're brilliant at, that you love and make a mint at it.'

There was a hard edge to her voice that didn't quite gel with what she was saying.

'You have a remarkable way of saying something must be fantastic in a way that makes it sound a bit crap,' he said.

She glanced up at that and gave him a you've-got-me smile.

More genuine this time. A shrug.

'I'm sorry. I didn't mean to sound jaded. A few years working in the hotel industry does that for a person. It's hard graft with horrible hours at times, and the pay isn't great.'

There was an undertone of bitterness in her voice.

'It hasn't always been that easy for me you know,' he said. 'And to be perfectly honest it has its downside even now. I mean look at me, having my freedom curbed this week because of the tabloid interest. I didn't sign up for fame, I signed up for the tennis.'

'You've certainly made the most of the fame side of it though, haven't you?' she remarked, a cynical tilt to her chin that he couldn't fail to miss. 'I mean if you wanted to concentrate purely on the game you could lead a quiet life, keep yourself out of the public eye, maybe not pose half naked in women's magazines...'

'Ah that.'

'Yes, that.' She pointed at him with her fork. 'You can't put yourself out there, courting publicity, dating a different woman every week, and then moan when public interest bites you on the arse. Why exactly *are* you on house arrest again?'

It wasn't intended as a question and he knew from her cynical expression that she'd read the papers. He felt on shifting ground with her and it was a sensation he wasn't used to when it came to women. There was no easy admiration to be garnered from her. He knew she was attracted to him, it was obvious in the way she stole glances at him, in the sharp intake of her breath when he moved close to her, but apparently attraction wasn't enough. He had the oddest feeling that there was an element of contempt for him lurking beneath the polite surface conversation and he was irritated by his irrational compulsion to find out why. Why should he care what she thought of him? He didn't *do* that kind of concern. She was a welcome distraction for the week to prevent him staring at these four walls. No point making it any more than that.

He held his hands up.

'OK, OK, so I've made the most of the perks of being in the

public eye, I'm not denying that. I just didn't expect it to interfere with my sponsorship and my game.'

The familiar stab of resentment spiked in his gut. He'd had one dodgy tournament, knocked out in the first round by an unknown. A fluke, nothing more. An off-day. It certainly had nothing to do with the fact he'd gone to a party in the previous days, something that would never have been an issue if the girl he ended up with hadn't blabbed full details to the press. It hadn't even been the night before the game, he would never have done that. And yet still he was being treated like a wayward teenager. And frankly, he was used to a bit less criticism and a bit more fawning from the girls he had dinner with.

He put his fork down and leaned back in his chair.

'How come you're so unimpressed by me, so uninterested in the whole success and fame thing? I've never met anyone so dismissive of it, you actually seem to go out of your way to make a point of it.'

She burst out laughing.

'Used to people watching you adoringly and falling over your every word, are you?'

He grinned back.

'Actually, yes.'

'Celebrity rubbish doesn't have that effect on me I'm afraid. It's all totally shallow. I prefer to stay rooted in the real world.' Then she shrugged and backtracked a little as if realising she was being insulting. 'Nothing personal, though, I'd had a gutful of the celebrity fishbowl way before I ever met you.'

Just what the hell did that mean? He frowned at her.

'How do you mean? You make a habit of bursting into unsuspecting celebrities' hotel rooms?'

'No. I try to make a habit of NEVER doing anything like that,' she said, and added '*Ever*,' as if he wouldn't get the point.

'I don't follow.'

He waited patiently, unfazed by the silence, letting it drive her to elaborate.

'My mother is currently working her way across America with my savings, following some insane has-been rock group who've decided to reform,' she said. 'I only found out when she went AWOL yesterday and it took me a whole day of trying before she picked up her phone at the airport. In her head she's still eighteen and wearing leather trousers. It's completely tragic.'

'Rock group?'

She nodded.

'I was absolutely furious and yet and at the same time not entirely surprised.'

The look of tired resignation on her face for some reason tugged at his heart.

'Why not? She make a habit of that kind of thing?'

He couldn't imagine having a parent like that. His own straight-down-the-line mother and father flashed into his mind. Paragons of respectability. Hard to live up to.

'She spent the better part of my childhood doing exactly the same thing.' She gave him an I-don't-care smile that was a bit too small to really pull off.

'Travelling?'

'With a purpose.' She eyed him for a moment as if deciding whether to keep talking, then shrugged. 'She's the number one fan of this ageing Glam Rock eighties band. She spent months travelling, went to every gig they ever did back in the day, and now they've decided to get back together. I saw it all the first time around. They might've been able to pull off eyeliner and big hair twenty years ago but now they just look like a tragic bunch of middle-aged saddos who really need to grow up.'

'So your mother is a groupie?' He bit his lip hard but failed to stop a smile. At least now he knew her cynical attitude had nothing to do with dislike of him. And when she was talking seriously about something she had a determined tilt to her chin which was the cutest thing he'd ever seen.

'No, worse than that. She's an ageing groupie. Go on, laugh

it up, I can see you want to. And it *is* funny. Or it would be if it wasn't so bloody embarrassing.' She shrugged, obviously thinking of her lost savings. 'Or so bloody expensive. Reforming old bands is the order of the day, there's this big eighties revival going on, but of course what it's really all about for them is making a fast buck. Problem is, all the fans got old too. My mother no longer fits the bill of cute groupie, not that it stops her.'

He groped for something to say that wouldn't sound like he was taking the piss.

'What about your father?' he managed.

She speared a cherry tomato with her fork.

'From the same kind of universe I'm afraid. He was the lead singer in a one-hit-wonder rock group. If I told you their name you might even recognise it.' She paused. 'Then again, maybe not. You were probably in nappies when they were at the height of their fame.'

'I'd never have pinned you as having such an unconventional upbringing,' he said. 'You seem so focused on your job, so sensible, and you look so...' he searched for the right words '...not like a rock chick.'

Oh yes that just sounded great.

'Yeah well,' she said, taking a sip of her champagne. 'The clue's in the name.'

He frowned, thinking it over.

'*Layla*?' he said. 'You mean like—'

'The song. Yep. My father's all-time favourite. If only he could have been that talented, eh?'

She was very good at not taking herself seriously, it was impossible not to like her, with her jokey self-deprecating description of her background, yet there was a barbed edge to her tone that told him that however outwardly amusing all this might be, in reality for her it was anything but.

'Are they still together, your parents?'

She shook her head.

'He never lived with us. It was just some backstage fling my mother had. Not sure either of them had counted on me as a consequence. He sends Christmas cards. He's a cinema manager now of all bloody things, somewhere up North. I have an address. But I've never had a real relationship with him. Nothing to do with my parents has ever been real. For all my mother's obsessing, it's never led to anything concrete. That money she took would have been my deposit on my own little place. She might as well have just thrown it off the plane. It will just be frittered away; there'll be nothing to show for it.' She took a sip of her wine, looked at him over the rim of the glass. 'I don't expect you to get that, you're clearly someone who's had an excellent return on their hard work but that's because it's YOUR celebrity, YOUR success. My mother thinks that hanging around that will somehow make it rub off on her and in reality the opposite is true – all it ever does is bleed her dry. And now me too.'

Their backgrounds were wildly different yet he could relate so easily to that feeling of not being the focus of his parents' life, of somehow not being enough to satisfy them.

That odd feeling that she was fighting not to like him now made perfect sense. She kept herself consciously detached, he could see her doing it, making small talk, keeping her professional image going, yet in the moments when he broke through that barrier it was clear she was as attracted to him as he was to her. The fact drew him to her even further. She liked him in spite of his status and image, not *because* of it, and that to him was intoxicating.

Layla pushed her plate away, half finished, the beautifully presented meal pushed thoroughly into a haphazard pile that would have given the Michelin-starred chef palpitations. She'd said too much. Given away far too much of herself. Yet she'd had no real opportunity to vent her building fury at her mother, and once she'd started it was hard to stop the outpouring of bitterness. Maybe the fact he was from the same shallow world added to it. He was the perfect by-proxy target for her exasperation. Part of her felt better for letting off steam, yet her plans to keep things professional had somehow been forgotten in the process.

'How did you get started then?' she said. If they were going to talk family background, let it be about his no-doubt perfect one instead of her own train wreck of a childhood. She sat back in her chair and sized him up. 'I bet you were one of the kids in sports lessons at school who got to pick the teams, weren't you? I was the one lurking at the back because the whole picking process was hideous. Either that or I wouldn't be there because I'd accidentally-on-purpose forgotten my kit.'

He grinned and nodded.

'Sport not your thing then?'

'Two left feet, zero co-ordination. Do you come from a sporty family?'

She imagined him as a kid smashing a tennis ball around a court while his family looked on proudly.

He took a sip of champagne.

'Not really,' he said, not looking at her. 'In fact I probably couldn't come from a less sporty family. My parents are both academics.'

She thought she picked up a hint of guard about his tone, but that couldn't be right, could it? This was small talk, of the most general kind.

'Really?'

'My father's passion is medieval history. He's written a few books, he's quite highly regarded in that field, if medieval history's your thing. With my mother it's English Literature.'

'Wow,' she said, impressed. Her own mother, for whom work was an irritation to be avoided whenever possible, had dropped out of school before managing any qualifications.

'I know,' he said, clearly picking up on the awe in her voice. 'I'm not sure they knew what to make of a kid who couldn't master basic grammar and had no aptitude for math. I wanted to spend every waking moment outside. Then I discovered tennis and there was no going back. Suddenly there was something I was good at after all.'

The bitter edge to his voice was hard to miss.

'They can't be disappointed by your achievements, surely. You just chose a different path to them, that's all.'

He shrugged.

'My brother and sister are a lot more intellectual than me. Emma is a teacher and Will is a research scientist, high up in his field. My parents can probably relate to that kind of achievement a bit more. I was adopted so growing up that was a bit of a thing for me, I wanted to be the same, fit in with the rest of my family. I wanted to be the academic kid who could do the math.'

He was concentrating on refilling her glass, not looking at her. She felt a pang of unexpected sympathy for him. She knew a lot about trying to make an impression on your family, she'd spent her childhood not knowing where she was going wrong with that.

'Don't misunderstand me,' he said. 'They're pleased I've done well. They just have no passion for tennis themselves. There's none of this father-as-coach stuff.' He sat back in his chair. 'What was your thing at school then, if it wasn't sport?'

'Nothing was particularly my thing.'

'There must be something. Everyone is good at something.'

'I had a bit of a talent for playing guitar,' she said dismissively. Oh the hideous irony of it.

'Had?'

'My father taught me when I was very young.' She took an ill-judged big sip of her champagne and tried not to cough. 'One of the only positive inputs he's had on my life actually. I don't really play anymore though, haven't picked up a guitar in years.'

Her father's interest had petered out after he left. She hadn't seen the point of playing after that, without a hope of his approval to encourage her. Certainly not as a way of following his example and chasing fame. She couldn't think of anything worse.

She felt an odd sense of affinity with Matt Stanton, of all bloody people, which was totally ridiculous of course because their lives couldn't be more different as it stood right now. Yet were their backgrounds really that far apart? He'd struggled to find a way of being good enough for his family's approval. And she wasn't sure she would ever find one.

***

A fire sparked and crackled in the hearth. Dinner over with, she stood and crossed to the fireplace to add another log, then took the lighter gadget from the mantelpiece and moved around the room touching candles alight, straightening the brocade cushions. *Working*, he realised.

'Leave that,' he said. 'Come and sit down.'

She hesitated before picking her half full glass from the table and following him across the room. He noticed that she waited for him to sit down before she followed suit, and then she took the opposite sofa. On her guard. Yet he'd felt a fleeting touch of something closer when they were talking over dinner. He couldn't remember being so intrigued by someone, and her reticence only served to interest him even further. She was such a welcome foil to the one-sided conversations and endless bubbling enthusiasm of the usual girls he mixed with.

Her skin was honeyed porcelain in the flickering firelight, her hair gleaming. The baby pink softness of her upper lip made him itch to take it between his own lips and suck, just to see if it still felt as delectable as it had yesterday. Low burning began to course through his body just from looking at her.

Layla could feel his eyes on her and when she looked up from her glass the way he caught and held her gaze in his said it all. Her pulse rate made a break for it and her stomach melted to soft heat. An anticipatory tingle rose in her breasts and between her thighs at the thought of his hands on her, the memory of what had happened between them not twenty four hours ago in this suite crashing through her barriers straight back into her mind. The evening was theirs for the taking and he made his move by standing up, rounding the low coffee table and sitting beside her to take her hand in his.

She looked down at it.

'I told you before, I'm not some fangirl. I know that sounds ludicrous after what happened yesterday, but that was *so* not what it was about for me.'

'What was it about then?'

She considered the question, not sure she really knew the answer.

'I don't know. Proving a point maybe? Perhaps I'd just had a gutful of playing by the rules for once. Working, savings accounts, behaving responsibly…really it's got me nowhere in life. My mother running out was the last straw.' She shrugged. 'I just wanted some fun.'

'You regret it?'

The deliciousness of the previous evening danced through her mind.

'Yes,' she said, meaning no.

She was a crap liar. She saw it in his smile.

'You're like a palate cleanser,' he said. 'A reality check in the middle of all the madness.'

A single word or move from her would be enough to revert this whole situation to platonic. She simply needed to make herself and her position clear once again.

She didn't withdraw her hand. Somewhere in the depths of her mind lurked the dark and delicious urge to take this further, this crazy situation she'd got herself into. Not just take it further but run with it, as far as she could. Maybe there was some kind of inevitability about her attraction to him that made it undeniable. Could this be an opportunity to explore her mother's crazy lifestyle, to somehow get a tiny bit closer to understanding her parents and her own dysfunctional upbringing? Why not experiment with that world a bit herself? It didn't mean she was going to fall for him, she had her head screwed on far too tightly for that.

That was the difference here, *that* was what set her apart from run-of-the-mill groupie. She had an agenda of her own that wasn't about fan worship.

Or was she actually just clutching at straws to justify this to herself when it went against everything she'd always believed? Was she really considering continuing with this madness?

The thought made her stand up quickly, and she moved back towards the table, began stacking dishes on the silver trolley to be taken downstairs.

'Thank you for dinner,' she said over one shoulder. 'But it's getting late, I should think about finishing up here.'

She forced her mouth to say the words and when she had finished up here she would force her feet to walk out of the door.

And then he was behind her, one arm curling softly around her waist and the other sweeping her hair to one side so he could kiss her neck. Sparks fizzed down her spine as he turned her to face him and she looked into those melting dark eyes and felt rationality dissolve. She slid her palms slowly up his taut chest, feeling the hard muscle again beneath the fabric of his shirt, before sinking her fingers into his hair.

His hands slipped to the nape of her neck, his thumbs grazing her jawline softly as he tilted her face to the perfect angle and caught her lips with his, the softest most featherlight kiss.

And then he stopped, put a little space between them. Her heart raced in her chest. Acquiescence – that was what he was looking for. Some sign after her attempt to back off that really she wanted this too. All this talk about his childhood and the way he seemed to court the attention of the press – there was an inherent need for validation in everything he did, why would this be any different?

Her heart was pounding, desire racing through her veins at his touch, her mind insisting it meant nothing even as she moved powerlessly to close the gap between them. Rationalisation would have to come later now, she was beyond that presence of mind.

She stood on tiptoe, leaned in and touched his lips lightly with her own. That one tiny movement was enough. He swept her against him, his mouth groping for hers, forcing it open, caressing her with his tongue. Her hands went to the buttons of his shirt, his slid down her body, lifting her skirt, rucking it up to waist height.

The urgency was intoxicating. His mouth hard against her neck, he tugged at her panties and she wriggled free of them and kicked them away. And then he was lifting her, his hands sliding beneath her bottom, her legs locking behind his back, her shoes still on her feet. He grabbed the half-full champagne bottle from the table as he passed and carried her across the suite and into the bedroom, kissing her as he went. Then she was lowered onto the bed, the softness of the sheet beneath her back and shoulders as he slipped each garment off her, kissing her skin as he exposed it. Naked now, she watched him strip off his own clothes, her breath coming in short bursts, sweet anticipation fluttering in her stomach.

He tugged her legs to pull her close against him at the edge of the bed, and she could feel the hard press of his arousal against her. An eagerness to explore him, to explore every delicious sensation to its full overtook her, and she reached down to stroke him, to caress the velvet softness of his skin with her fingertips. He moaned against her neck as she found a rhythm and the sound thrilled her, that she could invoke that kind of response in him.

He caught her hands in his and held them at her sides, kissing her softly on the mouth, his breathing harried against her lips. Desire fizzed in her stomach as he deepened his kiss and eased her backwards until her shoulders sank into the bed. Looming above her, he trailed kisses from her mouth, soft against her jaw, and down until he closed his lips over a nipple. He sucked gently, teasing her nipples with his tongue, cupping her breasts in his palms and holding them close together so he could easily access first one and then the other, his tongue slipping softly across the erect tips.

As he slid two fingers inside her, she let out a helpless moan

of pleasure, and eyes closed, she felt him smile against her neck. .
She opened her eyes as he pulled away a little, in time to see him
drink from the bottle of champagne and hold the golden liquid
in his mouth, and then he was leaning down and parting her
thighs to expose her completely. A momentary bolt of shyness
at his sigh of satisfaction and then she drew breath sharply as he
leaned forward and closed his mouth over her swollen core. Icy
champagne fizzed against her oversensitised skin, his tongue cold
against her, and the sudden hard deliciousness as he sucked her
dry made her throw her head back to gasp at the ceiling. He held
her against his mouth as her body writhed, eking out every final
second of her satisfaction.

A brief moment to lie spent on the softness of the bed as he
reached for a condom, and then he was easing her legs apart with
his own. She felt his length, big and hard as he rubbed it slowly
between her legs, teasing her until she so ached to feel him inside
her that she resorted to begging for it. And when she thought
she could stand to wait no more, he finally acquiesced, thrusting
forward smoothly in one hard, fluid movement, right to the hilt,
stretching and filling her completely. Lifting her feet, one heel
in each hand, he pulled them to his shoulders as he moved, the
resulting deep hard thrust of him making her gasp and clutch
the sheet. She spiralled toward dizzying heights of pleasure as he
took her with hard, full strokes, his hands reaching forward now
to cup her breasts, the nipples teased tight between his fingers,
pulling her into his arms in the final moments to crush his mouth
to hers and moan his own sated pleasure against her neck as he
took them both over the edge.

****

Somewhere during the last two hours her legs had turned to jelly.
And how she thought she could go back downstairs and carry on
with work as per usual, she had no idea. She sat up and glanced

at her reflection in the gilt edged mirror on the opposite wall. Her hair was one big tangle, and her makeup – what was left of it – was smudged beneath her eyes. She looked – and felt – like sin. And what shocked her the most was that there was a part of her that absolutely revelled in it.

She tried, with the rational part of her mind that hadn't been completely seduced by the most unbelievable sexual experience, to think clearly. Her body was toast. She'd never known intimacy like it. But then of course he'd had a ton of practice, knew exactly what buttons to press to please a woman. He only had to brush against her to start the heat fizzing again right to her toes. She would have to rely on her head to get her out of this. Easing herself inch by careful inch, so as not to wake him, she edged towards the side of the bed and still lying down, put one foot out of it onto the floor. She moved a little more until she was hanging on the bed by one elbow and one bum cheek, poised to swing herself up and out. From there she'd thought no further than tracking down her clothes. Maybe once she'd got them on and tidied herself up she could figure out what to do. The corner of the sheet held in one hand ready to throw back, she gathered momentum, and then he suddenly sat up next to her in the bed.

CHAPTER SIX

He was looking down at her, torso on the bed, head still on the pillow, but hips over the side and feet touching the floor, eyebrows raised, an amused expression on his face, and she knew from the heat of embarrassment in her cheeks that she now had a bright red face to add to the birds nest hair and slutty make up. Just bloody perfect. She couldn't even pull off a swift exit without stuffing it up. Then again, maybe she took after her mother, for whom swift exits weren't an option when it came to men. Outstaying your welcome was more her thing.

'I need a shower,' she said stiffly. 'And then I need to act like I've done nothing this evening except work.'

She sat up quickly and crossed the room to the ensuite bathroom, the crumpled sheet clamped against her body to hide her modesty, not caring that he'd explored every inch of her in the last few hours. The sheet unwound itself from him and the bed as she tugged it after her and when she glanced back he was lying back on the pillows watching her, that little half-smile on his lips that made her stomach melt like toffee, arms behind his head, his tanned and toned body completely naked in all its strong gorgeousness. Her heart leapt into full gallop and heat bloomed in her cheeks as she rounded the corner into the bathroom at full speed.

She could no longer write this off as a mad moment. There

was no heated phone call with her mother to blame this time for her impulsiveness. In fact, could something even *be* impulsive if you did it more than once?

She leaned her boiling cheek against the cool tile wall. She was NOT about to fall for him. She absolutely wasn't. What this was – if it was actually anything at all – was an inconsequential fling. If what Lucy had said was anything to go by, she'd just joined the ranks of normality, nothing more. And could it really do that much harm? Couldn't she even see it as a way of gaining some much-needed insight into the world her mother populated? She'd never understood her mother's behaviour, had never managed an easy relationship with her. Maybe this could be a way of slaying some demons.

Her mind was halfway to being convinced, her body was already there. It would be so easy to just talk herself into carrying on with this because the beauty of it was that she already *knew* how it would end. That fact in itself made the risk so much more palatable. She could be certain that she was in control of this situation because she knew *exactly* what she was getting into here, both in terms of intimacy and time frame. It would be done with by the end of the week. She knew how he operated – she'd read it a hundred times in different gossip magazines or newspapers. Read about one of his flings and you read about them all – once you made it into his bed, it wouldn't be long before you made it back out of it. If you were savvy and had no personal scruples, you might get a one off cash bonus for your trouble if you sold your soul to one of the tabloids. You wouldn't be the first. Women meant nothing to him. He was the epitome of bachelor playboy.

And if she told herself that over and over, she might erase the lingering doubt that churned in her stomach that, actually, she was in serious danger of losing her heart here.

***

She left the room and his mood plummeted. And then dropped a notch further again in dismay that he was actually bothered. When had there last been someone in his bed – or his life – who'd made that kind of impact? For Chrissake the hardest part usually was *getting* them to leave, sometimes even strong hints weren't enough and he had to resort to bringing in security. None of that with her.

Sex with her was unbelievable, an exploration, the way she slowly yielded to him, the way she delighted in new sensation, her eagerness to throw herself one hundred per cent into every moment. But there was something alluring about her that didn't just show up in the sack. Top of the list was her indifference to his fame and his success that at times seemed to border on contempt, coupled with the fact that she was attracted to him in spite of it. His celebrity had no pull for her, if anything it was a turn-off. If she slept with him, she did it because she couldn't help herself, because she liked *him*, not the trappings associated with him. That kind of validation was so fresh and different, it seduced him. She was addictive.

And now she was apparently leaving. Again.

***

She glanced around the bathroom. How many times had she been in here to check everything was perfect? Always thinking wistfully that she would never get the chance to use anything this nice herself. There was a huge open plan rainforest shower, underfloor heating and fluffy towels. The hot tub nestled in the opposite corner. She deliberately avoided looking in the huge mirror over the his-n-hers sinks, knowing her hair would belie exactly what she'd been doing for half the night. Instead she turned the shower on and stepped under it, letting the cascade of water soak her hair and run over her skin. She pawed through the array of complimentary toiletries on the shower shelf, of which she intended to use the entire collection. Deciding on orange and bergamot shampoo, she tipped a generous puddle of it into her palm and began to lather her hair, rinsing off the bubbles, closing her eyes against the warm water.

And then from nowhere he slid into the shower beside her, and any tentative resolve she was kidding herself was still in place melted like the soap on her skin.

Matt slid his hands around her, over smooth skin slick with bubbles and warm water, the fresh citrus scent of the shampoo filling the steamy air. The glide of her hands up and over his chest had a sensuousness to it that staggered him. Hot desire flooded his veins as she smoothed her hands slowly over his skin. He found her mouth with his and moulded her wet body tightly against his as the kiss deepened. She tasted faintly of toothpaste and she felt like heaven.

He found her nipples with his fingers, cupping her breasts softly in his palms and rolling the hard tips between his thumb and forefinger, applying pressure softly, then with increasing firmness. He felt the response in her body, in the way she gasped and clutched at his soaking shoulders. That he could thrill her like that caused a surge of desire so hot and intense that he wanted her immediately, and he slipped his hands to her waist with no thought beyond possessing her completely.

And then she was covering his hands with hers and pushing him gently until his back hit the cold tile of the wall. Taking control away, making his senses reel. The shower spray missed his face now, poured instead in a flowing torrent over his lower body, and the scented steam misted the air as she sank to her knees, her fingertips trailing down his torso, the very light touch of them making muscles and nerves jump and flutter in his groin. Her touch was slow, deliberately so, her fingers sliding firmly around his hard length, her other hand moving lower to cup his balls. And then her mouth slipped sweetly over the head of his rigid shaft and he heard a deep moan of pleasure escape his own throat.

She touched him on a deep visceral level that he hadn't known existed. The water sluiced over his lower body, soaking her hair and hands. Heedless of it, he was able only to think of that delectable contact, all other thoughts crushed from his brain by the sweet delicious friction. She sucked gently, her tongue caressing him lightly, driving him maddeningly fast to that edge of pleasure, yet as if she had the ability to read his mind she adjusted her movements to keep him hovering at that pinnacle until a surge of animalistic base desire rushed his mind. Before he could lose the final threads of self-control he pulled her roughly to her feet, knowing nothing except that he had to have her right now, no more diversions.

He carried her from the shower room, water trailing in puddles across the tiles and then soaking into the deep carpet behind them, the shower thundering on in the empty bathroom. In a couple of swift movements he had her on the bed, water soaking slowly into the sheet beneath her from dripping skin and hair. Groping for her mouth with his, he kissed her, parting her lips with his tongue, the better to taste and caress her. Her nipples were hard points against his chest, her legs like silk wrapped around him as he pressed between her legs, pushing straight inside her, hard and urgent, wanting to possess her completely, unable to wait. Her gasping moan of pleasure spiked his arousal even further and then he screwed her slow and deep, both his hands tangled in her hair, holding back his own satisfaction until he could push her to that plane of delight. As he felt her tense beneath him, he let go of his own restraint to spiral over into that delicious pleasure as she cried her ecstasy into his mouth.

***

Once was a blip.

Twice was a slip.

Three times was to gain some insight or understanding of her parents, specifically her mother.

Four times was just for the hell of it – she'd done it now, the damage was done, once more wouldn't make things any worse. Plus she needed his good reference when he finally checked out, it was her fastpass to promotion, no point in pissing him off by stopping now when she'd already slept with him anyway.

How many times would she need to have sex with him before all other possible justifications were used up and she had to admit this was really about wanting him and nothing else?

The week had been punctuated by days of throwing herself into her work while Matt focused on his training sessions and physio meetings and whatever else he got up to. Afternoons and early evenings together, always in his suite, sometimes sharing dinner, sometimes talking, always ending up in bed before she left him for the night and made her way back to her grotty shared accommodation.

And now just a couple of days left before he checked out and she was lying in bed with him in the middle of the afternoon, knowing she had no ulterior motive left for being there. Somewhere in the course of the week it had simply become about being with him. Each day a step closer to all of this ending, something she'd always known was inevitable.

For the first time ever she'd had a glimpse of what the intoxicating pull was for her mother in the unreality of this current situation. Why wouldn't she want to live on the fringes of some fantasy when reality was so mind-numbingly dull? There was something addictive about that, wasn't there?

Yet it shouldn't count for much in the face of your family or your kids. And Layla had always had that perspective that her mother lacked. Give it a few days and it would be over, he would be gone, back to the States and the tennis circuit and his fabulous celebrity life. And *that* was where Layla would prove herself as better. There would be no following Matt Stanton around the world to gurn at him from the stands at this tournament or that match, no hanging on the meagre crumbs of interaction he might throw her way when his exciting life got back to normal.

Making that point clear to him might be the best way of cementing it in her mind, of maybe putting a stop to the growing churn of sadness in her stomach that she was trying to ignore.

'Only a couple of days and you'll be heading on back to the States,' she began, sitting up and hugging her knees with her arms.

'Yup.' He was watching her, eyes slightly narrowed. Guarded. What was he expecting, her best fangirl don't-say-it's-over speech? He must be expecting that at some point, right? She took a deep breath.

'You don't need to worry,' she said. 'I'm not about to cast myself at your feet when you check out and beg you to keep seeing me.'

Matt lay back against the pillows, arms above his head and smiled at the determined tilt to her chin, the steady holding of his gaze with her own. He hadn't let himself contemplate the end of the week. Why would he? He'd had many, many flings before, all of them live-in-the-moment. When it was over he simply walked away without looking back, why would he see this situation as any different?

'You're not?'

She shook her head.

'No. I'm sure you've had your share of women doing that but it isn't going to happen this time. We've always known this wasn't going to last beyond the week so I'm hardly going to be expecting you to invite me to the players' box at your next match or dedicate your next big win to me.'

He sat up straighter. She was really pressing the point here and her lack of interest really should be an advantage, right? The last thing he needed was a messy ending to all this when he checked out. So why did his stomach suddenly feel like she'd kicked him in it?

'What makes you so sure I won't do exactly that?' he said.

She gave him an incredulous grin.

'Matt, your record speaks for itself. You date a different girl every week. Nobody lasts. You and I have ended up like this because for one week only, I've been your only option. It was me or pay-per-view, right? We both know this is just a quick fling. It doesn't mean anything. Outside this suite there's a whole different world. Our paths would never have crossed and if they had neither of us would have looked twice at the other.'

Her indifference felt like a knockback, despite the fact he hadn't been serious about the tickets and the Grand Slam dedication. She leaned over and kissed him briefly on the mouth, just that one contact firing him right back up again, before sitting back up again. The natural reaction would be to tug her back down into bed with him and see where the rest of the afternoon might take them.

Instead he took a long look at her, the smile in her blue eyes, her messy blonde hair, that delectable top lip that he just wanted to kiss and kiss.

His mood had taken an inexplicable nosedive and on impulse he threw the covers back, making a snap decision that would be dismissed as crazy if he let his mind think it over for longer than a second. Why risk it? Why bother when he had sex on tap in this suite with no risk of trouble from his management?

Because suddenly her opinion seemed to count more than any of that. He wanted to be more to her than some throwaway fling for the week.

He stood up and turned on the main light. She looked up at him from the bed, the sheet pooled around her waist, long legs drawn up and a questioning expression on her face.

'What are you doing?'

He held his hand out to her.

'Taking you out. Come on.'

She stared at him.

'You don't need to do that just to prove a point.'

'I'm not. I'm going stir crazy in here. Get dressed. Do you have a coat?'

He tugged her by the hand until she swung out of the bed and stood up.

'Yes…but where are we going? What if you get recognised? I thought you were meant to be keeping a low profile.'

He held up a hand.

'The thing about being recognised is not to hang out where you might be expected to.'

CHAPTER SEVEN

Matt Stanton's attempt at incognito apparently amounted to a dark blue hooded jacket. Then again, he didn't really *do* incognito that often from what she'd seen in the press, so it made sense that he didn't really have a clue when it came to disguise. He was obviously planning to keep his head down and hope for the best.

She trailed after him as he slammed the door behind them and strode ahead down the corridor, the unreality of being out of the suite with him adding to the madness, shrugging her jacket and scarf on over her uniform as she walked. She came to a standstill as he reached the foot of the staircase and turned towards the lobby and the glass revolving front door, complete with nosey concierge to one side of it.

'I can't be seen leaving the hotel on some jaunt with you,' she called after him in a stage-whisper. 'I'll get the sack.'

He glanced back at her.

'Why does it have to be a jaunt – as you call it? Why can't it be work related? You're meant to be working for me after all. Leave it with me.'

Before she could stop him he'd marched up to the reception desk and informed the duty manager that she would be providing admin support off the premises at an afternoon meeting, and then before she knew it they were outside on the cold pavement.

The weather was winter crisp and the air was icy clear in her throat as she breathed in, puffing out in a soft cloud as she exhaled. There might be an hour or so of proper light left before the last faint shards of winter sunshine disappeared and dusk took a hold. She was conscious of his hand holding her cold fingers tightly as they walked along the pavement. His zip up jacket couldn't conceal his broad muscular frame although its hood partially hid his face. But surely all it would take was a second glance from a passer-by to blow his cover. He seemed completely unfazed by the prospect and her heart gave a tentative skip. Was this some sign that he wanted more from her than a week of fun? Surely he wouldn't be this laid back about being seen with her if she really was as dispensable as that, especially with the press intrusion he'd had recently. The whole world was waiting for him to slip up again.

'Where are we going?'

Her stomach was a knot of tension. She knew perfectly well the kind of place he liked to frequent. It would be some buzzing bar or other, some celebrity haunt where tourists went to spot famous faces.

'Not far. Just far enough to escape and get some fresh air. And some space.' He dodged people and traffic like a pro and eventually tugged her into Hyde Park.

He tucked Layla's hand into his own as they walked, stopping off at a food stand to buy them a steaming coffee each. The air had a fresh clarity to it and the open space was a welcome change. As he looked around them at the frosty grass and the trees, bare of leaves now, golden sunlight slanting through their branches, he realised for the first time that he'd spent most of the last week indoors. Even when he was training much of it had been gym based. No wonder he'd felt hemmed in – this normality was the kind of thing he really missed out on, the freedom to do what you choose and go where you pleased had a value all of its own.

Who knew that this kind of simplicity could be so intoxicating? Hot coffee, open space and her company. As they reached a circular fountain, she let go of his hand and climbed onto the stone lip of it, arms outstretched, coffee cup in one hand.

'I wasn't expecting the park,' she called down to him and the smile on her face made his heart flip softly over.

His eyes were drawn to her as she put one foot in front of the other in her sensible court shoes, clearly intent on completing a circuit, and he bit back a smile as he followed her lead, hopping up and beginning to walk the fountain himself in the opposite direction. The water below looked deep green and very cold.

'What *were* you expecting?' he called across to her.

She paused in her journey, arms outstretched but not a hint of wobble, nose crinkled in a very cute thoughtful expression.

'Some bar I suppose,' she said. 'Whenever I see you in the papers you're always falling out of some swanky celebrity nightspot or other.'

'And are you disappointed then? With the choice of venue?'

She started walking again. Coming towards him now, a full circle nearly completed. He stood still and waited for her to reach him, then stepped down onto the frosty ground and lifted her gently down and against him, his arms finding her waist and sliding around her.

'Nope,' she said, her cheeks pink with the cold. 'It's perfect. I haven't been to the park for ages. I work all hours, it's lovely to get some fresh air.'

He kept an arm around her and headed for a bench at the side of the path. She sat down next to him and took a sip of her coffee.

'Most girls I meet are falling over themselves to go to a club or a restaurant with me,' he said. 'And you're happy with coffee and jumping around a fountain.'

She smiled up at him, her eyes sparkly and the tip of her nose pink in the cold. He wanted to kiss it.

'You're too used to women swooning over you,' she said. 'I guess some people really are that shallow, that they're so impressed by the image or stories they see in the press they have no regard for what the actual person is like behind the headlines. Because you look amazing when you take your shirt off on court and you're rich and you have these impetuous arguments with umpires and bed models and starlets, people don't look any deeper than that.'

'Except for you.'

'That kind of thing doesn't impress me,' she said, taking the lid off her cup. Steam curled from it as she took a sip, watching him over the rim of the cup. 'I guess I'm just not like most girls.'

'No,' he said, holding her blue gaze with his own. 'You're certainly not.'

The way he looked at her made her stomach melt. Her heart give a joyful little skip in her chest and she immediately checked it. Somehow that seemed so much harder to do with him alone out here in the cold air, with none of his rich-and-famous trappings buoying him up. He was bucking stereotype by bringing her here. And she'd been relying on that concrete stereotype as justification for keeping her emotions in check. Suddenly it felt a little as if she were standing on uncertain ground.

When he took her coffee cup from her and set it on the ground next to his own she didn't stop him. He tugged her onto his lap and she couldn't help herself snuggling into him. He smelled faintly of aftershave, deep woody notes, and the jersey of his hoodie was soft against her cheek. He tilted his head down and found her mouth with his, holding her tightly against him, his arms curled around her back, one hand finding and stroking her hair. The kiss was slow, lingering and deep and she could taste the faint twist of strong coffee on his tongue. There was something gentle in the way he held her, the way he stroked a stray tendril of hair away from her face and tucked it behind her ear, the way he caressed her cheek. This felt somehow more intimate than even the hottest moments they'd spent back in the hotel room.

He'd risked going outside to prove some kind of point and now he was cuddling up to her in public, not that there were many people about, a few joggers, but still. Heat flowed slowly through her veins to pool in her stomach and she swallowed hard. But there was a part of her desperately wanting to make all this significant. Surely if all he wanted was a quick and easy lay he would never have suggested leaving the hotel?

With dusk on the brink they began walking back. Sparks began to simmer deep inside her, a want to get him back to the hotel suite, to have him all to herself in private again, the physical desire for him so strong it shocked her. He caught her hand in his as they walked and she looked down at that physical connection, biting her lip hard enough to hurt. This should not mean anything to her. It certainly shouldn't be reducing her insides to melted chocolate. But it had been a hell of a lot easier to dismiss this as just an experimental take-it-or-leave-it fling before he had to bring touchy-feely *affection* to the bloody table.

They were out of the park now and back onto the cold pavement. Early evening London traffic pushed its way past them, the street lights beginning to kick in. A light mist began to fall around them, softening headlights and clinging to her hair. And then a group of three young women approached them, giggling and chatting, and Layla saw rather than felt the sudden double-take as one of them clocked just who it was they were walking past.

'Matt *Stanton*?' Narrowed eyes and swooning beatific smile kicked in instantly on the woman's face.

Matt stopped and dropped her hand like a stone. The intimate connection broken in an instant, without so much as a thought. And her eyes, tuned in to pick up every detail in magnified sharp clarity, noticed him put a couple of paces between them. He was withdrawing his contact with her. She was dismissed. That's how it felt. That's what it was. And for Pete's sake, had she *really* imagined he would behave any differently?

She added another pace backwards herself as he turned to the women, instant smile lighting up his face, ready and willing to meet his adoring public.

'Omigod I'm such a fan, you have no idea,' one of them was

babbling. 'I sleep on the pavement every year at Wimbledon. I'm first in the queue to watch you play.'

'That's really very sweet.'

She heard the smile in his voice. Her stomach churned hideously. Not one of them acknowledged that she was there. Why would they? Matt hadn't acknowledged her, if anything he'd made it clear she meant nothing to him in the face of their adulation.

Really, what did she expect? To be introduced to them as his girlfriend?

Furious with herself, she watched the second girl, slim and attractive with blonde hair piled messily up on her head, tugging her jacket off and undoing the top buttons of her blouse with one hand. With the other she fumbled a pen from her bag and pressed it into Matt's hand.

'Can I have your autograph?' she said, tugging her blouse apart and thrusting a pink-bra-clad breast at him.

Matt took the pen from her with a flourish as much giggling ensued.

An unexpected wave of nausea rose in Layla's throat and she pressed a hand to her mouth and blinked hard to clear her watering eyes. There was no way she was staying to take in another second of this and she turned away to head back to the hotel on her own. Unfortunately not before she picked up the breathy cry of gratitude, 'I'm never going to wash again!'

Classy.

***

She retouched her make up in the staff toilets, removing all trace of kissed-off lippy, and kneeled underneath the hand drier briefly to blast away the damp from the misty rain. As if by restoring herself to work mode she could somehow undo her epic unprofessional behaviour this week. She should never have let any of this happen, it had been utter madness. She'd let herself be sucked into seeing

75

him as a real person with proper scruples and genuine emotions, when in truth his image was always going to come first. Every aspect of his behaviour was influenced by it, she saw that now.

A wake-up call. And not before time. What the hell had she been thinking, letting herself get involved with someone like him?

Lurking beneath the hideous disappointment was fury with herself because she was even bothered. That was somehow worst of all. She'd thought herself so above all this, had believed she was immune to the charm of someone like him. Turned out, she was no different to every other female with a pulse.

Still, better late than never. All she needed to do now was avoid him. Make some excuse, maybe get one of the butlers to cover for her. He was scheduled to check out in forty eight hours, how hard could that be?

***

'Kerry Suite's just called down,' the manager said as she emerged from the toilets directly into his path. Layla's hands instantly crept to smooth her shirt into place, as if he might still somehow guess that work for her this week had had little or nothing to do with, well, actual *work*.

'Apparently you're meant to be there?' He frowned. 'Some kind of admin task, ring a bell?'

Admin task? Oh just bloody perfect.

'I'm really tied up here,' she gabbled, taking a step away from him in the direction of the kitchen. 'Maybe one of the concierge team could step in?'

The frown morphed into raised eyebrows. 'I thought you were able to handle this,' he said. 'Can't just chop and change the point of contact for the guest. We committed to letting him use you as staff for the week. That comes first. Whatever you're tied up with here, get someone else to do it. Unless you're not up to the job of course. Which,' he added pointedly, 'would be a shame with the departmental changes in the pipeline. You're hardly recommending yourself for the post here are you? If you can't pull out all stops for one guest, we're hardly going to believe you can do it for a hotel full of them.'

She changed direction and headed for the lift.

***

She took a deep breath outside the door before giving it her standard work double-tap. Her heart might be thundering like a train but she rearranged her face into what she hoped was a detached professional expression.

He opened the door. She could see beyond him that the fire had been lit. Its mellow glow lit the sitting room area cosily. The mist of their walk had turned into full on rain now, she could hear it pattering at the windows. His smile of welcome made her stomach churn. So he was back in his suite with the rest of the world shut out and now she had a place. In his bed, to be precise. She'd had a glimpse now of what it would be like when he checked out of the hotel. No place for her in any of that. The disappointment twisting in her stomach told her that somewhere deep down she had hoped that wouldn't be the case, that there could somehow be more for them after this week, however hard she might have denied it to herself.

'Where did you go?' he said.

'Was there something I could help you with?' she said, talking over him loudly. 'I got your message.' Oh yes. She'd well and truly got *that*. 'Some kind of admin task was it? Because I'm not sure now that I'm the best person to meet your needs for the rest of your stay.'

He opened his mouth to speak and she held up a hand to stop him.

'I'm not going to leave you in the lurch, you needn't worry. I can make sure one of the concierge team is available for you twenty four hours. Or possibly a butler, if that's more the service you're looking for.'

He stared at her as if she were an alien.

'I don't want some concierge or butler. Why would I? I'm perfectly happy with the present arrangement.'

Something inside her snapped.

'That's exactly what this is, isn't it? An arrangement. I should never have let it get this far.'

'What are you talking about?'

She gestured madly between them.

'This. Us. You and me. I should never have let things get personal. I should have just gone with my first instincts and kept things between us professional. And I definitely should never have gone out with you.'

A sudden flash of clear understanding burst into Matt's mind as she cut her gaze away from his. So that was what this was about. The fans they'd come across. Seriously, it wasn't as if he'd been mobbed. It was three women.

'You were jealous.' he said in surprise. For some reason the prospect of that gave him a spike of happiness. For all her maddening indifference she *liked* him. This proved it. Her furious denial proved it even further.

'I am NOT jealous!' she snapped. 'I am NOT some sad groupie. What I *am* is disappointed that there actually *isn't* more to you than lucrative sponsorship, crazy publicity and screaming fans.' She lowered her voice then, as if she was reigning herself in.

'Of course there's more to me than that, but that's what people want from me, Layla. My sponsorship deals, my fan base, all that has come from raising my public profile, and that comes from interacting with the public, being seen in the press. Do you really think I'd have the kudos and success that I do if I kept my head down and never put myself into the limelight? This is the way things are. All I did was sign a couple of autographs and pose for a picture, you're talking like we were mobbed. I just don't understand what the big deal is.'

He cast exasperated eyes at the ceiling. Just the fact he was arguing this point was new territory for him. In his usual remit, he'd be letting her walk out the door, possibly with a flash of gratitude that he'd had a lucky escape from such high maintenance grief. 'This is my life, Layla. This is what it's like. None of it's *real*, none of it *counts*. Not on any level that matters at least.'

He took her elbow gently and turned her back to face him, but she wouldn't meet his eyes. She looked down at his hand on her arm, her lips pressed together so hard that they were white.

'We were talking, Matt,' she said. 'Mucking about in the park, getting to know each other. Those things are real, normal. Those things are worth spending time on. And then a gaggle of women clock who you are and the moment's over. I might as well have not even been there. You were swept up in their adulation before I had a chance to draw breath. Well I have absolutely no desire to be anyone's second best, left shuffling from one foot to the other in the background, waiting until you get bored with the praise being heaped on you and remember that I'm actually there.'

Exasperation began to rise in his chest as he held her frowning, angry gaze with his own.

'I like the real you,' she said quietly. 'The one who was at the park, the one who talks about normal things, who told me a bit about his childhood.'

Her refusal to listen to him made his temper break free, not least because he felt her regard for him slipping away and he had no idea how to regain it when the one thing that he'd always relied on to impress people happened to be the one thing she really wasn't impressed by.

'Being with you these last few days hasn't only been about sex, you know.' He shrugged and conceded, 'OK well, it might have started out that way but as I've got to know you it's turned into something else.'

'You would say that of course,' the coldness didn't waver. 'Say the right things, whatever works to get me into bed, isn't that right?'

He couldn't stop an incredulous laugh. Did she really think he would be bothered with her insane high maintenance if the only thing he liked about her was sex?

'Has it not occurred to you that the reason I like being with you is because you DON'T ask me to autograph your tits?' he snapped. 'If sex was all I wanted I'd say *Layla, you're not needed anymore* and I'd call up one of a dozen or so women I know in London who'd be happy to provide just that. Or I would have invited autograph girl back here for the evening.' He flung exasperated hands up. 'Do you think I don't wish it could be that straightforward? Like I need this grief! Nothing about you is easy, you're impossible to impress, you change your mind every five minutes and you think the worst of me by default. But for some crazy reason the only person I want to be with right now is you.'

He paused for breath as she stared at him, roused out of her coldness by his raised voice and exasperated tone. He made a monumental effort to calm down.

'You're the first person I've met who isn't impressed by who I am and that's new territory for me.' He ran his hands distractedly through his hair. 'I've spent my life trying to impress and that's what got me where I am. I *can't* just dispense with that side of my life. It's who I am, Layla. It's made me what I am.'

And without it he really wasn't sure who he was. Or whether he would be good enough for her or for anyone.

Her heart turned softly over at the anguish in his face. Not to mention the fact that he'd just compared her to the celebrity fishbowl and she'd come out on top. OK so he'd also said she was difficult but she could overlook that in the light of the overall sentiment.

Could she really let herself believe there might be something more to this than a throwaway week? How that could possibly play out going forward, she had no idea, but for now just knowing he thought she was different was enough.

She raised her hand and for a split second he thought she was about to slap his face. Nothing would surprise him coming from her, wasn't that what the whole appeal was? Instead she touched his cheek softly with her palm, her blue eyes softening. He covered her hand immediately with his own, lacing his fingers through hers, holding her gaze in his. And then he pulled her close and kissed her.

Lingering kisses this time, a chance to taste, feel, caress. As she melted against him she slid her arms up to curl around his neck and then he was lifting her, carrying her, kissing his way across the suite to the bedroom where he lowered her onto the softness of the bed. Removing her clothes was a delight to be lingered over, every inch of her skin his to kiss until she was squirming deliciously under his hands.

He savoured the silk of her skin against his and her gasp of pleasure as he slid inside her thrilled him. With each long smooth stroke into her he breathed in the sweet scent of her hair, savoured the delectable softness of her lips against his. The caress of her fingertips on his skin and the satin of her legs as she curled them around his back, pressing him deeper into her as her breathing rose, her soft cries of pleasure against his shoulder, these things thrilled him on a deep level he'd never known before. The want, the *need* for her was so strong, so all-encompassing that it shocked him to the core as he pushed them both towards the point of ecstasy. Sex had never been about this for him. It was about self-gratification, appreciation, emotions need not apply. He didn't *do* sex with emotional strings.

Breathing began to level. He looked into the china blue eyes below his as she held his gaze steadily with her own, pupils dilated, and felt a connection to her that seemed to fill his every sense, something that forced rationalism out of the room.

This was no take it or leave it fuck, and he'd been kidding himself that he could somehow pass it off as such. When he bedded a girl it was fast, fun, a means to a very pleasurable end.

He considered their enjoyment of course, made sure he gave as good as he got, but it had never given him such pleasure to please someone before. Her every sigh of delight spiked him with a surge of happiness. He'd never felt this desire to get to know someone before, beyond the physical, her hopes and dreams, her past. All the things that made her tick. It was new territory and it filled him with tentative hope and happiness.

She fitted into the crook of his arm as if he were made just for her. As their breathing evened, the caress of his hand against her back became slower, languorous, loving even, and she tried to memorise exactly how the moment felt so she could revisit it in her mind later when she was alone.

'Why is it such a big deal for you?' she said idly, holding his hand in hers, examining his palm. 'The worship I mean. The media hype. Isn't the sporting success on its own enough? Lots of celebrities moan about press intrusion but you seem to lap up the attention.'

She thought she felt him tense a little against her.

'Everyone has an angle, don't they?' he said. 'It's just happened that way for me. It helps with sponsorship having a high media profile.'

His voice sounded guarded and she pulled away enough so she could see his face and raised a sceptical eyebrow at him. They both knew he was fobbing her off with that answer. He sighed.

'The honest answer, I guess, is that I've liked it. I didn't impress like that when I was growing up. With my brother and sister wiping the floor with me grade-wise I felt more and more like an outsider.' He paused briefly, as if considering whether to keep talking. 'And the adoption, Layla. My family have been great, I've always felt loved by them and I've never wanted for anything, but still at the back of my mind there's always been this knowledge that someone rejected me once. For someone, I wasn't good enough. And the tennis success, the interest that came with it, that felt like the answer to everything. Finally I was good at something and the fan stuff, well that continued to prove it. And for a young red-blooded guy with a full on academic upbringing that he could never quite pull off, the female interest was like a gift. You can't blame me for taking advantage of it.' He squeezed her shoulders. 'I haven't told anyone this stuff before. I'm not even sure I've thought it through myself.'

'Why are you telling me this now?'

Her heart was thundering in her chest. His singling her out, the personal talk, all of it made her spirits soar and her guard lower.

'Because this week with you, it's the first time I've haven't had someone's admiration off pat. Your approval has nothing to do with my tennis or my image and it feels good.' There was surprise in his voice. 'It feels different.' He paused long enough for her to think he was done, and then from nowhere, 'And I don't want that feeling to end.'

***

This was no disposable fling, it had somehow crept into being a whole lot more. The hotel stay was the reason, he saw that now. He'd never have had the chance to spend so much time with her in the whirlwind that was his real life. Yet the wave of happiness that rose up now had an undertow of fear. He could feel it there, lurking, ready to tug him under. Right on the heels of the euphoria came something else – self-doubt and fear, because when time had been added into the equation and novelty value had gone, what was left had never been enough to impress anyone else. And Layla hated all things celebrity – just look at her reaction today over a couple of fans. How long would this last before she realised it was all hype? That underneath he wasn't all that?

He wasn't sure he could face finding that out.

***

83

Their last day together. And after yesterday was she so wrong for hoping there could be more to them now than just this week or two? Exactly what, she had no idea. But they could figure it out. Hope fluttered in her stomach no matter how hard she tried to squash it and she was all fingers and thumbs as she dressed in her uniform and took the Tube across London, arriving early for her shift, eager to see him.

The manager swooped in like an overweight vulture as she crossed the lobby.

'Ah, Layla. Change of plan today. If you could start by checking the Kerry Suite over, making sure Housekeeping have done a good job. We've got a last minute booking coming in, couple of nights only, arriving later today.'

'But the Kerry Suite's occupied,' she said. 'The current guest doesn't check out until tomorrow morning.' She avoided saying Matt's name. She couldn't trust herself not to smile at the sound of it.

'He's checked out,' the manager said, a congratulatory grin on his face as the bottom fell out of her stomach. Her face must have given her away because he reached across the counter and gave her upper arm a comforting squeeze. 'No need to look so worried, it isn't a problem. Something about preparing for his next tournament, he had to leave a little earlier than expected.' He leaned in conspiratorially and winked at her. 'Not before he left you a glowing reference though. Should stand you in brilliant stead for the managerial vacancy. Nice job.'

Nice job? Despite all her good intentions she'd dared to think he might feel the same, and the measure of the week they'd spent was 'nice job'?

She backed away from him as he turned to speak to a passing guest and left the lobby before the sudden ache in her heart could become anything more obvious.

In a dream she made her way up to the top floor, half wondering if there might be some mistake and that he would be there with his lopsided smile waiting for her, knowing in the wrenching depths of her stomach that he wouldn't be.

On autopilot she walked through the empty suite, straightening cushions, checking the final touches, the same way she had just over a week ago when Matt had checked in. The room was back to its perfect self. Not one trace remained, not a single hint that the past week had ever happened. Which was clearly how Matt wanted it. It might never have happened at all but for the desperate sensation of sinking in the pit of her stomach that bravado alone just wasn't enough to suppress.

It hurt. Hurt deep down in her gut. And the rejection really wasn't the worst part of it. It was the stupidity. Her own stupid pride, letting herself believe that he was interested in her on some level beyond his usual take-it-or-leave-it. What shred of evidence did she have that she was appealing enough to change him? For Pete's sake he'd been with women a hundred times more attractive than she was. She'd seen it over and over in the papers. Models, starlets. If he hadn't changed his attitude for any of them he wasn't about to break stereotype for dull as dishwater Layla Jones, who hadn't even been lovable enough to keep her own mother ditching her in favour of some pipe dream. What hope could she possibly have had with someone like Matt if she couldn't even hold the interest of a blood relative?

CHAPTER EIGHT

Sleep had given way to a more pressing need to give herself the talking-to of her life. And with limbs aching and eyes scratchy from tiredness, she turned up for her shift the following morning. Back to daytime hours now. No need to be here afternoon and evening to provide entertainment anymore. The thought made her catch her breath and she swallowed hard, concentrating on staying focused.

Fortunately she had the prospect of a new job to latch onto.

The manager gestured to her practically the moment she walked into the lobby. Obviously wanting to discuss the new post, he'd virtually said it was as good as hers the previous day. She followed him into his office, trying to muster some positivity when all she wanted to do was hide back in her studio flat and sleep the pain and humiliation away.

OK so she'd made a total fool of herself over Matt Stanton but it wasn't as if her life was over. In the process she had actually kept him happy for the week, and OK it might feel cheap but he'd given the management a glowing report. She might not have bagged the rich tennis player, but let's face facts, that was never really on the cards anyway, and at least she'd bagged the promotion. She could look forward instead of back, perhaps start cautiously looking for a new flat, somewhere of her own where she could finally put down roots.

Maybe, if she tried hard enough, that thought might actually start to make her feel better sometime soon. This decade would be good.

She waited, modest smile on her face, almost hearing the congratulatory words before he spoke them, ready to accept her consolation prize.

He gestured at the seat opposite his desk.

'Sit down.'

He didn't look particularly congratulatory. Then again he'd always been a bit dour. Decades of working in the hospitality industry could do that to a person, she could easily believe it. Still, she liked to think that when she gave the employees on her team good news, which she would soon be in a position to do with her new title of Guest Services Manager, she'd give it to them with a bit more of a happy attitude than this.

He clasped his hands together in front of him on the desk.

'It's come to my attention that you've been acting outside your remit this past week,' he said.

The words were so unexpected that she gaped at him.

'Excuse me?'

'Your actions with a certain high-profile guest may have been a bit less than professional. And anyone who works here, particularly in Guest Services, where you're required to work closely with guests, must be absolutely beyond reproach.'

He pressed his lips together and looked at her with an expectant don't-make-me-spell-it-out look on his face.

She made him spell it out.

'In what way? I've done everything I was asked to do. You told me yourself the guest was perfectly happy when he checked out.' She couldn't bring herself to say his name in case her hideous disappointment took over and buried her.

He leaned forward awkwardly, his own face reddening now.

'You were *seen*,' he said. 'In some kind of clinch in a public park. The most high-profile guest we've had in months and you were draped over him on a park bench. Have you any idea how this makes the hotel look?"

'You're wrong,' she said, stabbing an obstinate finger at him. Denial. That was her only chance. What proof could he possibly have?

'There's a mobile phone picture of you with him in this morning's paper,' he said, grabbing a copy of one of the red-tops from the side of his desk and thrusting it at her. 'One of the Reception staff just gave it to me.'

On the front page was a grainy, but perfectly clear to anyone who knew her, photo. Herself on Matt's lap in the park, when he'd kissed her until she thought she might dissolve into a puddle. Faint gratitude surfaced amid the shock that they hadn't actually gone any further than kissing, though they'd certainly been on the brink of it. His words fell on her like stones.

'The gossip among the staff is at fever pitch. Are you really going to tell me nothing went on between you?' he snapped. 'Clearly you're having some kind of relationship with him.'

She knew when she was bang to rights.

'I'm not going to tell you nothing went on,' she said. 'I'm just saying it couldn't have been less like a relationship. And you definitely should be using *past tense* when you talk about it.'

***

For Matt walking away had seemed the smart move and it hadn't even been that hard. He was so used to moving on that initially it had been nothing short of automatic.

Then reality had kicked in and with it a sense of loss that made his stomach churn and his mind and body ache.

Even then he'd thought this dwelling on her would be short-lived. But now it had been nearly a month and she was still invading his every waking moment with her sweet smile and her funny, sparky attitude.

His tennis was at its best. The Davis Cup was coming up soon and he'd thrown all his energies into preparing for it, believing that was all he needed to move on. A distraction. Especially needed now because distractions of the other kind seemed to have quit working for him. Oh he'd been out a couple of times when he got back to the States, believing he could slip effortlessly into his old exciting lifestyle. His week with Layla Jones would be quickly forgotten.

Instead the opposite seemed to be happening. Partying held no appeal. Girls threw themselves at him the same way they always had but now his mind seemed to constantly compare them to Layla, and the constant adulation and fawning made him impatient and irritable. His interest in getting laid had dwindled to nothing. At this rate he'd have to start living in a cave, emerging only for matches.

He'd thought all he'd need to do was give it time and everything would be back to normal.

Just how much bloody time was it going to take?

***

'Just to say I got your message about the job and the change of address. And you needn't worry about me, darling.'

'I wasn't.'

Layla put the phone down briefly on the sticky carpet while she sellotaped shut the last box.

No boyfriend. No mother. No job.

And now nowhere to live. Without regular income and no savings to fall back on, there was no way she could keep up with the rent on her studio, however grotty it might be. The only thing left to do was pack. When she picked the phone back up her mother was still talking.

'...going to be staying on in the States for now. The band have added a few extra dates to the end of the tour and I'm sharing a truck with one of the roadies.'

Layla's stomach gave a churn at the thought. So the celebrity rock and roll dream was still alive and well for her mother then. Still, one faint glimmer of positivity in the gloom – by the time her mother resurfaced Matt Stanton would be a distant memory and she'd never need to know about her daughter's disastrous fling with fame.

'Great,' she said.

'Well you could sound a bit more enthusiastic,' her mother said. 'I don't know why you're so depressed over this job. No social life, awful pay. You shouldn't be seeing this as a knockback, you should be seeing this as an *opportunity*.'

Layla failed to stop a cynical laugh.

'If you hadn't disappeared with my savings I wouldn't be needing an *opportunity*. I'd have enough money to tide me over.'

Her mother made a dismissive chuffing sound because of course, she was never wrong.

'You'd be back in the mind-numbing workplace before you knew it. Trust me, Layla, this could be a good thing. It forces you to step outside the box for once. You've got no ties, you're free to go your own way. Why not wing it for a while and see where life takes you?'

For some reason the thought didn't fill her with horror anymore in the way it always had. Focused on making her own security in life, saving up for her own place, she'd kept her eye on the prize so closely that she hadn't noticed the journey to get there was anything but fun. The hotel job had been hard graft, hideous hours for little thanks and low pay.

Her mother clearly took her silence as encouragement and swept on.

'Sometimes the best things in life are things you do on impulse. If you question the hell out of every decision you make, it stands to reason that you'll talk yourself out of trying new things.'

A long held dream slipped unexpectedly into Layla's mind,

forged during a school trip to France what felt like a lifetime ago. She'd loved it, had told herself she'd come back one day when she was older, maybe take in some more of Europe along the way. A dream that had been lost in the ensuing years when her life had become more and more unstable and she'd directed everything she had at steadying it. There'd been no place in her mad quest for stability for things like travel or adventure. Maybe, though it stuck in her craw to say it, her mother might actually have a point for once.

'You could fly out and join me. Check out the band. What do you think?'

Maybe not *that* kind of adventure.

***

Lucy had offered her a sofa until she got back on her feet but the way things looked that wasn't likely to be anytime soon. From management material to sofa surfer all because of one crazy week. That was what you got from being seduced by a celebrity, and she only had herself to blame because of all people, she should have known better.

There'd been a hideous few days after she'd got the sack where paparazzi had hovered around the front door hoping for a picture or a quote for them to spin out yet another story about Matt Stanton. She'd had handwritten notes from journalists shoved under the door offering to let her tell her side of the story. She'd kept expecting her mother to turn up at any moment, rucksack in hand, ready to take control and bask in the attention. That she hadn't was the one aspect of the whole sorry mess that had gone Layla's way. And in time, without a new angle, the journalists had given up and left her alone. On to the next disposable story.

Her phone rang as she stacked her stuff in the corner of Lucy's sitting room. Six boxes and a couple of bin liners, that was what her life amounted to. She checked the screen.

91

'Lucy,' she said, picking up. Obviously checking she was settling in.

'Where are you? At the flat? Turn on the TV. News Channel.'

The television was only feet away from her new home. She sat on Lucy's sofa and flicked it on.

'Why?'

Speech trailed away. She saw why. And a new lurch of despair churned its way into her stomach, just when she thought she got it under some kind of control.

'Oh cheers for this,' she snapped, finding her voice. 'The guy has single handedly cost me my job and my home. Why the hell would I want to watch him earn millions on the sodding tennis court?'

His face filled the screen and the broken remains of her heart apparently still had a bit of flip left in them. He looked as gorgeous as ever, hair tousled and damp with sweat from whatever match he'd clearly just won, judging by the euphoric squeals of the crowd behind him. So he'd got his form back then. Well lucky, lucky him. Her life was in tatters and his was right back on track.

A microphone was thrust at his face, the TV interviewer fawning her congratulations over him. He only looked at her. There was none of the usual playing to the cameras. She'd seen him interviewed countless times in her former life as mere tennis fan and he wasn't above kissing interviewers on the cheek or climbing over crowds to the player's box to celebrate a win with his team. Lobbing shirts into the crowd was par for the course. But this time there was no cheeky smile on his face, and no flirt in the brown eyes.

He thanked people for their support in the deep American drawl that she constantly tried to block from her mind. Now he was graciously praising his opponent. And then his face blurred and she blinked furiously and reached for the off button.

Thanks, Lucy. Trying to expunge him from my mind and you present me with that.

'And I'd like to dedicate this win to someone very special to me...'

His face disappeared into blackness as she failed to stop her finger hitting the switch.

'Fuck!'

A single dazed moment as she realised what she'd done and then she attacked the remote control. And from there ensued an enormous scramble as she turned the thing back on and waited for it to bloody well warm up only to find that the sports bulletin had moved on to sodding golf. And from there five crazy endless minutes while her heart pounded and her mind spun and she waited for her laptop to boot up so she could find the piece online, and during which she convinced herself that the someone very special to him would be his sister, or an aunt or…and finally, there it was.

'…Layla Jones. This is for you. I'll see you soon.'

CHAPTER NINE

'You saw my interview, after the win in Paris?'

He perched on the edge of the two-seater sofa in Lucy's flat, mug of coffee in hand, having had his telephone offer to fly her out to Paris rejected. Even now she continued to surprise him. This was the first time he'd seen her wearing anything other than her staid hotel uniform, and in her pink T-shirt and boyfriend jeans with her hair in loose waves instead of the sleek professional style she favoured at work, there was an unspoilt quality about her that made his stomach heat up.

Shame about the icy expression on her face. Clearly if he'd thought declaring she was special to the world at large would be enough to make up for his, admittedly crass, quick exit a month or so earlier, he'd seriously underestimated her resolve.

No sign of any support from him when her life had imploded and she'd had to turn her phone off to stop the endless stream of journalist calls, but now he wanted to see her again! She'd had no intention of lifting a finger to go to him. She'd had enough of having her hopes lifted only to be dashed the moment she took her eye off the ball. If he wanted to make amends that badly, he could damn well come to her.

Not that it wouldn't have been nice to join him at the touted five star luxury hotel. But principles were principles.

'I saw it,' she said dismissively, as if she hadn't rewound it fifty times and downloaded it to her phone. 'And if you think that's enough to make up for your behaviour, you are so wrong.'

Her stomach still melted at the sight of him. Broad, tanned, tall, same tousle to his hair, same brown eyes. He wasn't smiling, which was a good thing. If he'd swanned back in here as if he'd done nothing wrong she might have been tempted to lob her coffee cup at his head.

He ran a hand through his hair and shifted uncomfortably in his seat.

'I'm sorry.'

'Course you are. It's just taken you nigh on a month to get round to saying it.' She looked down at her mug, anything to avoid looking at the tortured expression on his face. It was so much easier to keep channelling the upper hand by picturing him smugly checking out of the hotel without saying goodbye. 'I lost my job, Matt. I've been *evicted*. Do you know what that means? Can't imagine you do since you probably own a house on every continent.'

The widening of his eyes told her he had no idea how things had gone for her after he'd left. She was at her lowest point, jobless and sofa surfing at her friend's house, and he'd clearly jetted out of the country without a second thought to what might happen to her.

'Oh yes,' she said, relishing his horrified expression. 'Just when I'd got my head round the revelation that what happened between us really *was* just a seedy fling, despite all the things you said to me, I'm dragged through the press, I lose my job and on the back of that I lose the flat.'

'It wasn't seedy. Please don't say that.'

'Are you sure about that? Because it didn't warrant any kind of explanation before you just took off, did it? What happened to things being different with me? It was all just sweet talk after all, to get what you wanted from me for the week.'

His face twisted as he shook his head.

'That's not true.'

She threw an exasperated hand up.

'Did you or did you not leave without saying goodbye?'

He cast his eyes downwards.

'It seemed the best thing.'

She gave a bitter laugh which he totally ignored.

'I want us to be together,' he said. 'You and me. What do you say?'

Her heart gave a skippy jolt but she kept a hold on it. She'd been hurt too badly to just wave a hand and let things slide.

'It can never work,' she said.

'Why not?'

'I've got plans,' she evaded.

'You're living on your mate's sofa with no job,' he pointed out.

'This is just a stop-gap,' she said, ignoring the plummet in her stomach that happened every time she thought of her current situation. 'I've decided to go travelling, just throw caution to the wind. I've got a little bit of money stashed from my last pay cheque – not much, but enough to give me a start, and then I figure I might try and work my way around Europe.' At least about that she was sure.

After the phone call with her mother, she'd seized the idea and run with it. 'I've spent years working hard and trying to have a normal life and it's got me nowhere.'

Winging it and living for the moment now seemed to have an appeal that it never had before. Within reason of course. She wouldn't be jumping into bed with anyone else at a moments' notice.

'Sounds good,' he said. 'Want company?'

Did he know how ludicrous that sounded?

'When I said I was going travelling, I didn't mean the insane kind of hero-worship travelling that my mother does,' she said. 'I'm not about to traipse around the world following you, if that's what you think, even if your career allowed for a fat sabbatical to go backpacking. You'd be mobbed everywhere you went.'

He closed his eyes briefly. Her determination to shoot down his every suggestion in flames was infuriating.

'I'm not an idiot. I know my tennis stands in the way of a lot of normal stuff. I know there will need to be compromises, but at least I'm trying to find some middle ground here.'

She was watching him, a vaguely sceptical expression on her face, but at least she'd stopped firing negatives at him.

'Travel with me,' he said. 'I want to be with you, Layla. Properly. Not just the occasional get-together when either of us has time or happens to be in the same place.'

The blue eyes widened.

'What about your celebrity love-in? You chose that over me once before. What's changed? What's so different now that I should believe you're not just going to get bored with me after five minutes?' She shook her head at him. 'Leaving me like that after what we had, what I *thought* we had…it had an air of inevitability about it, Matt. I don't even really blame you. Why would I? It's happened before. I might be an OK distraction for a while but when you put me up against fame and excitement I can't possibly compete. My father managed five years, drifting in and out of my life in between gigs, before he decided it wasn't worth the effort. My mother turns up every few months, and every time I fool myself into thinking she might stay put this time, start living a normal functioning life instead of some insane nomadic festival-obsessed existence. I've got it wrong every single time so far. I think it has novelty value for a few weeks, maybe a couple of months, the idea of actually being a mother, but after that she starts to get itchy feet and then before I know it she's off again.'

The defeated expression in her eyes made his heart twist in his chest.

'Why would I expect anything different from you? After all, for you the fame and the celebrity is real. All my parents ever did was ride on its coat tails.'

He grabbed her hand, frustration rising that he couldn't make her understand.

'You still don't get it do you?' he said urgently. 'The playboy image, the womanising. All of that is *what people see in me*. I don't let anyone know me beyond it because I know what would happen.' He lowered his voice. 'Behind all of it I don't measure up. I never have, not for anyone, not in any way that matters. I was scared that if you saw me for long enough for the gilt to rub off you'd lose interest. That's why I left, I thought I was doing you a favour, sparing us both a load of grief. The fame, the public persona, it's the only way I know to make myself count. But then when I walked away it just wasn't that simple. I just couldn't move on. I didn't want to move on, not without you.'

He held her blue gaze in his, knowing he needed to prove he was sincere.

'I told you a bit about my background before. You know I was adopted. I've always felt like a spare wheel in my family, however much they might love me. There's always been this feeling that someone gave me up. Someone rejected me once, for whatever reason. I look back at my behaviour and I've spent so much time over the years trying to make myself count, latching on to anything that made me feel worthwhile. The fans were all a part of that.'

'The truth is, I've lived this way for so long that without all the in-your-face public persona I'm not sure anymore who the hell I really am. And I was afraid that if I stripped away all of those things the person left wouldn't be worth an awful lot. And that…well, that wouldn't be good enough for you. You deserve so much more.'

Layla felt her resolve loosen as she took in the anguish in his eyes. It was just so hard to believe that someone with his success could feel anything but super-adequate in every corner of their life.

'But you're assuming that the reason you were put up for adoption had something to do with *you*,' she said. 'How could it be when you were just a baby? It was about circumstance. Haven't you ever tried to trace your real parents, look into it?'

Maybe that might have brought him some peace of mind.

He gave her a rueful smile.

'No. But a couple of years ago my birth mother found me.'

She stared at him in surprise, forgetting she was meant to be channelling cool and aloof.

'She did?'

'Only when I'd become famous. She never bothered before. I was only worth finding once I'd made it big.' He shook his head. 'As soon as I realised she'd only reappeared because she thought there might be a quick buck involved I cut all contact. I've never followed it up again since.'

There was bitterness and regret in his voice, and her heart went out to him for the terrible disappointment that must have been. She could see now that he was at his heart insecure, that his playboy behaviour had come not from any selfish drive but from his own feelings of inadequacy, and tears came pricklingly to her eyes because one thing she knew about was not feeling good enough or loveable enough.

'So what exactly are you suggesting?' she said doubtfully, and just the fact she showed some interest in any suggestion he might make felt like a victory. Hope kicked in, making his heart rate gather pace.

'If we keep seeing each other, where does your persona fit in to that? Are you planning on passing me off as a platonic friend? How exactly is that all going to work? Because you know the worst thing of all about this whole...' she paused briefly '...*affair* was that I can understand my mother's behaviour better now than I ever have. I can totally see how she could be sucked in by it year on year, going back to normality for a month or two before she gets itchy feet and necks off to some music festival or gig or other.' She took a deep breath. 'Because I feel like that about you. Part of me thinks I could put up with anything as long as I can keep you. I want to kid myself that I can do that, that I'll happily take whatever crumbs of your life are leftover once the matches and the partying and the socialising are over with. Because I want the lovely feeling to stay on that I have when I'm with you.'

His heart tried to soar at her words and yet the defeat on her face held him in check.

'I think I preferred it when I could take the moral high ground. When I didn't have that understanding and I could criticise her quite happily from my own safe standpoint of normality, with my career aspirations and my folders of interior decorating ideas and my mailing lists of houses. Suddenly that feels like the most mundane, most miserable existence in the universe. But I won't swop it for some half-life just because it means you'll be thrown in.'

He was on his knees at her feet, her small hands clasped in his, her blue eyes meeting his.

'Not some half-life. No partying, no crazy socialising, no groupies. I want to be with you. Properly. Not as some groupie or hanger-on. You travel with me, share my life, come to every game if you like. I'll reinvent myself as clean-living, no more posing in magazines or courting paparazzi.'

She looked into the melting brown eyes. He was ready to do all he could to be with her. And of course there was still risk involved, but still, how could she possibly come off worse than she already had? She'd already lost her job, her home and her heart. Stepping out of her comfort zone had never looked so attractive. What really did she have to lose?

Her mother's voice suddenly popped into her head.

Sometimes the best things in life are things you do on impulse.

'OK,' she said and then before she could elaborate she was in his arms, laughing with him, his hands everywhere, his mouth finding hers, desire bubbling through her and taking her breath away.

And it turned out sofas were good for something after all.